Also by Rachael Reed

Sis
Sis 2 Blood on the Streets

Standalone
Codefendant
Codefendant
Once a Cheater
Once a Cheater
Passport Bro
What Happens in Prison
Preference
Sprinkle Sprinkle
Championship Bad
Street Exodus
Street Exodus
Street Royalty
Pawns of Power
SIS
Cartel Bloodline
Get Money Girls
Skip the Games
Til Death Do Us Part

Demure
Diva

Check Out More Great Products and Free Giveaways

https://tbdbpublishing.com/

Chapter 1: The Good Girl

Carmen stood on the corner of Maple and 13th, her small, black purse clutched tight against her side. The bus was running late again, and she could feel the tension in the air. The sun was setting, casting long shadows across the cracked pavement. Around her, the streets buzzed with life—the distant blare of sirens, the rhythmic beat of hip-hop from a nearby car, and the occasional shout of kids playing tag. This was home. A place that felt both familiar and threatening, a place she'd known her whole life.

Carmen was a good girl. Everyone said so. Kept her head down, stayed out of trouble, worked hard at that accounting firm downtown. "Always on the grind," her mama would say with pride, her voice thick with a Southern drawl that hadn't left her since she moved up north. Carmen was always about her business, serious about her future. She had dreams, big ones. Night classes at the community college, working toward that CPA license. Her life was all about plans, structure, doing things right. No time for foolishness.

But this neighborhood? It was a different story. Ain't no plans or structure here. Just hustle. Folks trying to make it, any way they could. Carmen saw it every day on her way to the bus stop—the dope boys hanging on the corner, trading cash for drugs. She saw the look in their eyes, the hard edges. They was making their own way, but it wasn't her way.

Carmen's eyes drifted across the street to the boarded-up storefronts, the graffiti-splattered walls, the group of young men leaning against a dented Chevy. They eyed her as she stood waiting, and she looked away, her heart quickening. She wasn't scared—no, not exactly. But she was aware. Always aware.

"Yo, ma!" one of them called out, his voice slick with arrogance. "Where you goin' lookin' all fine like that?"

Carmen ignored him, keeping her gaze fixed on the empty road ahead. The last thing she needed was to get involved with the likes of him. Her mama always said, "You don't got no business wit' these street boys, Carmen. They gon' drag you down, girl. You got too much goin' on for that."

And she believed her. Carmen wanted more—more than what these streets had to offer, more than just scraping by, more than just surviving. She wanted to thrive, to make something of herself. She wanted out.

The bus finally rumbled up, its brakes squealing as it pulled to a stop. Carmen climbed aboard, flashing her pass at the driver, who nodded absently. She found a seat toward the back, pressing herself against the window. As the bus pulled away, she watched the neighborhood slide past, a blur of broken dreams and shattered hopes.

At the office, Carmen slipped into her desk and powered up her computer. The accounting firm was small, nothing fancy, but it was a job. It paid the bills, kept her mama off her back. And it was a stepping stone, a way to something better. She liked the order of it, the numbers that always added up, the neat rows and columns that made sense when nothing else did.

"Hey, Carmen," came a voice from behind her. She turned to see Linda, her coworker, a plump woman in her forties with a big smile and a bigger laugh. "How you doin' today, girl?"

"I'm good, Linda. Just gettin' started."

Linda chuckled. "You got that right, Carmen. Always standing on business. You doing better than most your age especially from that part of town you from."

Carmen shrugged, a tight smile on her lips. "Yea I gotta do what I gotta do."

Linda nodded, but her eyes were sympathetic. "Well, you keep doin' what you doin'. You're gonna do big things, I know it."

Carmen nodded, turning back to her screen. Linda meant well, but she didn't understand. How could she? She had a nice house in the suburbs, a husband with a steady job, kids in good schools. She didn't know what it was like to walk these streets, to feel the weight of them pressing down on you, squeezing you tight until you couldn't breathe.

After work, Carmen headed to her night class. The community college was a few stops down, and she made it just in time. The classroom was small, filled with other adults trying to better themselves. She took a seat near the front, pulling out her notebook and pen. This was her sanctuary, her escape. Here, she wasn't just some girl from the hood. She was a student, a future accountant. She was somebody.

The professor droned on about tax codes and deductions, but Carmen soaked it all in, scribbling notes furiously. This was her ticket out, her way up. She couldn't afford to mess it up. Not when so much was riding on it.

By the time she got home, it was late. The streets were quiet, the kind of quiet that felt heavy, like something was lurking just out of sight. Carmen hurried up the steps to her apartment building, the keys jingling in her hand. As she reached the door, she heard a shout from down the block—a man's voice, loud and angry, followed by the sound of glass breaking. Her heart leapt into her throat, and she fumbled with the keys, finally getting the door open and slipping inside.

Inside, it was dark and musty, the air thick with the smell of fried chicken and collard greens from Mrs. Johnson's apartment down the hall. Carmen's mama was sitting in the living room, watching one of her shows, the volume turned up loud to drown out the noise from outside.

"You late, girl," her mama said without looking up. "I was startin' to worry."

"I'm fine, Mama," Carmen replied, dropping her bag by the door. "Just had class."

Her mama nodded, her eyes glued to the TV. Carmen sighed, heading to her room. She closed the door behind her and leaned against it, closing her eyes. She could still hear the sounds from outside—the shouts, the sirens, the distant thud of bass from a passing car. This was her life, her world. A place where dreams went to die.

Carmen changed into her pajamas and crawled into bed, pulling the covers up to her chin. She stared at the ceiling, her mind racing. She thought about the numbers, the spreadsheets, the tax forms. She thought about her future, the life she wanted, the life she deserved. She thought about how far she'd come, and how far she still had to go.

She closed her eyes, willing herself to sleep. But sleep wouldn't come. Not tonight. Not with everything weighing on her mind, pressing down on her chest like a heavy stone.

She heard a knock at the door and jumped, her heart pounding. Who could it be at this hour? She glanced at the clock—11:30 PM. She got out of bed, her feet cold against the wooden floor, and crept to the door, pressing her ear against it.

Another knock, louder this time. "Carmen! It's me, Angela!" a voice hissed from the other side.

Carmen frowned, unlocking the door and opening it a crack. Angela, her neighborhood friend, stood in the hallway, her face pale and eyes wide with fear.

"Angie, what's wrong?" Carmen asked, opening the door wider.

Angela stepped inside, glancing over her shoulder. "It's bad, Carmen. Real bad. They got Devon. Cops all over. He got caught up in some mess, and they think he's the one who shot Rico."

Carmen's eyes widened. Devon was Angela's brother, always in trouble, always running with the wrong crowd. But Rico? He was one of the big players in the neighborhood, a shot-caller, someone you didn't mess with.

"Angie, what're you talkin' about? Devon ain't no killer."

Angela shook her head, tears streaming down her face. "Don't matter. They got him. Said he was at the scene. He's in for it now, Carmen. He's in for it good."

Carmen felt a chill run down her spine. This was the kind of thing that happened around here, the kind of thing that ruined lives, tore families apart. She reached out, pulling Angela into a tight hug. "We'll figure it out, Angie. Yall will get through this."

But even as she said it, Carmen knew things would never be the same. Not for Devon, not for Angela, and not for her. The streets had a way of changing people, of pulling them down into the darkness, no matter how hard they tried to fight it.

And as she held Angela in her arms, Carmen couldn't help but wonder if she'd ever truly escape the pull of the streets herself.

Chapter 2: The Unexpected Encounter

Carmen had just finished her shift at the accounting firm and was heading to the corner store to grab a few things before heading home. She kept her head down, focused on her own thoughts as she navigated the busy street. It had been a long day, and all she wanted was to grab her groceries and get out of there as quickly as possible.

As she walked into the store, she could feel the eyes on her. This wasn't unusual—she was used to the looks, the whispers. She was a pretty girl, after all, and she knew how men in the neighborhood acted. But she didn't have time for that today. She needed to get in and get out.

She made her way down the aisle, grabbing a carton of milk and a loaf of bread. She was reaching for a can of soup when she heard a loud, obnoxious voice behind her.

"Yo, ma! Lemme holla atchu for a minute."

Carmen froze. She knew better than to turn around. She could feel the heat of his gaze on her back, the weight of his eyes traveling up and down her body like she was some kinda piece of meat. She didn't need this. Not today.

She turned her head slightly, catching a glimpse of the guy out of the corner of her eye. He was tall, with a slick smile and a gold chain hanging from his neck. The kind of guy her mama warned her about. "No thank you," she said, trying to keep her voice steady.

But he wasn't taking no for an answer. "C'mon, girl. I jus' wanna talk to you," he insisted, stepping closer. "Ain't nobody tryin' to bother you or nothin'."

Carmen rolled her eyes and tried to sidestep him, but he blocked her path, his smile turning into a sneer. "I said, lemme holla atchu," he repeated, his voice low and threatening now.

She felt her heart start to race, her palms growing sweaty. She didn't want any trouble. She just wanted to get her groceries and go home. But it seemed like trouble had found her anyway.

Just as she was about to speak, a deep voice cut through the tension. "Ayo, back off, man. She said she ain't interested."

Carmen turned her head to see who had come to her rescue. He was standing in the doorway of the store, his arms crossed over his chest, a serious look on his face. He was tall, with broad shoulders and a confident stance. His clothes were expensive, the kind you didn't see much around here—designer jeans, a crisp white tee, and a leather jacket that looked like it cost more than her rent.

The guy bothering her took a step back, his eyes narrowing as he sized up the newcomer. "Yo, who the fuck you think you is?" he spat, his bravado faltering.

The newcomer didn't flinch. He just stepped forward, his eyes locked on the guy in front of him. "I'm the nigga tellin' you to step off," he said calmly, his voice low and dangerous. "Now get lost."

The guy hesitated for a moment, clearly trying to decide if this was a fight he wanted to pick. After a tense moment, he muttered something under his breath and slunk away, throwing one last glare over his shoulder as he left the store.

Carmen let out a breath she didn't realize she'd been holding, her heart still racing from the confrontation. She turned to her unexpected savior, her eyes wide with a mix of gratitude and curiosity. "Thank you," she said softly, her voice shaky. "I didn't know what I was gonna do."

The man smiled, and for the first time, she noticed how handsome he was. His skin was a rich brown, his eyes dark and intense. His smile was crooked, but in a way that made her feel like she was the only one in the room. "No need to thank me, ma. Just doin' what's right," he replied, his voice smooth and confident.

Carmen nodded, still feeling a little shaken. "I'm Carmen," she said, holding out her hand.

He took it, his grip firm and warm. "Travis," he said, his smile widening. "Nice to meet you, Carmen."

They stood there for a moment, just looking at each other. Carmen felt a strange pull in her chest, something she hadn't felt in a long time. There was something about Travis that drew her in, something magnetic and dangerous. She knew she should walk away, say thank you and leave it at that. But she couldn't. Not yet.

"You from around here?" she asked, trying to keep her voice casual.

Travis nodded, leaning against the counter. "Yeah, born and raised. But I been around, ya know? Seen some things, done some things. You?"

Carmen shrugged, feeling a little embarrassed. "Yeah, same. Well, kinda. I've lived here most my life, but I ain't really been nowhere. Too busy workin', I guess."

Travis nodded, his eyes never leaving hers. "That's good, though. Stayin' focused, keepin' your head on straight. Ain't a lotta people like that 'round here."

Carmen blushed, looking down at her feet. "I just... I got plans, ya know? Tryna do somethin' wit myself."

Travis smiled again, that crooked grin that made her heart skip a beat. "I like that, Carmen. I like a girl who knows what she wants."

Carmen felt a flutter in her stomach, a mix of excitement and fear. She knew she should be careful, that getting involved with someone like Travis could be trouble. But there was something about him, something she couldn't quite put her finger on. Something that made her want to take a chance.

"So, uh... you wanna maybe hang out sometime?" she blurted out before she could stop herself, immediately regretting it. What was she thinking? She didn't know this guy. He could be anybody.

But Travis just chuckled, clearly amused by her sudden boldness. "Yeah, I'd like that. Lemme get your number," he said, pulling out his phone.

Carmen hesitated for a moment, then took a deep breath and rattled off her number. What was the harm, right? It was just a number. Didn't mean nothin'.

Travis saved her number and slipped his phone back into his pocket. "Cool. I'll hit you up later, a'ight?"

Carmen nodded, a small smile playing on her lips. "Yeah, okay."

As she watched him walk out of the store, she felt a strange mix of emotions swirling in her chest. Excitement, fear, curiosity. She knew she should be cautious, that she shouldn't let herself get caught up in whatever Travis was offering. But at the same time, she couldn't deny the thrill she felt, the way her heart raced just thinking about him.

For the rest of the evening, Carmen couldn't get Travis out of her head. She replayed their encounter over and over, analyzing every word, every look. She knew she was being foolish, that she should focus on her work, her studies, her future. But it was hard.

Later that night, as she lay in bed, staring up at the ceiling, her phone buzzed on the nightstand. She reached for it, her heart skipping a beat when she saw Travis's name flash across the screen.

"Hey, it's Travis. Jus' wanted to say goodnight. Hope you dreamin' 'bout me."

Carmen felt a smile spread across her face, despite herself. She typed back a quick reply, her fingers trembling slightly. "Goodnight, Travis. Talk to you soon."

She put the phone down and rolled over, her mind racing. What was she doing? She knew better than to get involved with someone like Travis. She'd seen what happened to girls who got mixed up with guys like him. But at the same time, there was something about him, something that made her want to throw caution to the wind and see where this could go.

As she drifted off to sleep, she couldn't shake the feeling that she was standing on the edge of something big, something dangerous. And as much as she tried to convince herself otherwise, she knew deep down that she was already in too deep.

Chapter 3: The Chase Begins

Travis didn't waste no time. Right after that night in the corner store, he was on Carmen like a shadow, showin' up when she least expected it, always with that sly grin on his face. At first, she thought maybe it was just a one-time thing, somethin' to get her mind off the numbers and spreadsheets, but Travis wasn't like the other dudes in the neighborhood. He was persistent, like a dog with a bone, always pushin', never takin' no for an answer.

It started with the gifts. Flowers, at first. Roses, bright red and fresh, delivered right to her office with a little note that read, "Thinkin' of you, ma." Then, there was the jewelry. A gold bracelet, delicate and shiny, wrapped in a velvet box. Carmen had never seen somethin' so beautiful, let alone had someone buy it for her. She couldn't help but smile when she slipped it on, the cool metal against her skin.

Her coworkers noticed, of course. Linda, always nosy, cornered her one day by the coffee machine, her eyes wide with curiosity. "Girl, where you gettin' all this from?" she asked, nodding at the bracelet glinting on Carmen's wrist. "You got a secret admirer or somethin'?"

Carmen blushed, lookin' down at her shoes. "It's just... a friend," she mumbled, not sure why she felt the need to hide it. "He's nice, that's all."

Linda raised an eyebrow, her expression skeptical. "Nice, huh? Well, just be careful, Carmen. You know how these men are. They say they nice, then they turn around and—"

"I know, I know," Carmen interrupted, not wantin' to hear the rest. She knew Linda meant well, but she didn't need a lecture right now. Not when things were goin' so good. "I got it under control."

But deep down, she wasn't sure she did. Travis was like a whirlwind, sweepin' her off her feet, showin' her things she'd only ever dreamed about. Fancy dinners in restaurants with white tablecloths and waiters who spoke in hushed tones, their accents thick with some foreign flavor. He'd order for her, his voice smooth and confident, like he knew exactly what she wanted before she even did. She'd never been treated like that before, and it made her feel special, like she was the only girl in the world.

And Travis was always there, always ready with a smile and a joke, his eyes glittering with that dangerous edge. He'd show up at her job, leanin' against his slick black car, a cigarette danglin' from his lips. "Yo, beautiful," he'd call out when she stepped outside, his grin wide and mischievous. "Let me take you somewhere nice."

Carmen would hesitate, glancin' around nervously, feelin' the eyes of her coworkers on her. But she couldn't resist him, couldn't say no when he looked at her like that, like she was somethin' precious, somethin' he couldn't bear to lose.

But not everyone was so charmed by Travis. Her family, especially, was suspicious, always warnin' her about gettin' mixed up with the wrong crowd. Her mama, stern and worried, would pull her aside after dinner, her voice low and serious.

"Carmen, baby, I know you think you know what you doin', but you gotta be careful, ya hear? This Travis boy, he ain't no good. I can see it in his eyes. He's trouble, Carmen. Real trouble."

Carmen would roll her eyes, tryin' to brush it off, but she couldn't deny the worry in her mama's voice, the way her brow furrowed deep with concern. "Mama, it's not like that. Travis, he's... different. He cares about me, okay? He treats me good."

Her mama would sigh, shakin' her head, her eyes sad. "I just don't want you to get hurt, baby. You got so much goin' for you, so much potential. Don't throw it all away for some boy who don't care 'bout nothin' but himself."

Carmen would nod, pretendin' to understand, but inside, she was conflicted. She knew her mama was right, knew she should be focusin' on her studies, her career. But every time she thought about leavin'

Travis, about goin' back to her old life, she felt a pang of loss, a deep ache in her chest.

Her friends were no different. They'd whisper behind her back, their eyes full of judgment and disapproval. "Girl, you see what Carmen's been doin' lately?" one of them would say, her voice low and conspiratorial. "Hangin' out with that Travis fool. He's bad news, I'm tellin' you."

"Yeah, I heard he's got ties to the streets, runnin' with some real shady people," another would add, shakin' her head. "Carmen needs to wake up before it's too late."

Carmen would pretend not to hear, but their words cut deep, makin' her doubt herself, makin' her wonder if maybe they were right. Maybe she was makin' a mistake, lettin' herself get swept up in Travis's world. But then she'd see him, see the way he looked at her, like she was the most important person in the room, and all her doubts would melt away.

She knew she should walk away, knew she should focus on her future, on the life she'd worked so hard to build. But every time she tried, Travis would pull her back in, his charm and charisma too strong to resist.

One night, after another fancy dinner, he took her to a club downtown, the kind of place she'd only ever seen on TV. The music was loud, the bass thumpin' in her chest, the lights flashin' in time with the beat. Travis led her to a VIP booth, his hand on the small of her back, guidin' her through the crowd.

He ordered drinks, somethin' expensive and exotic, and they sat close together, his arm draped casually over her shoulder. Carmen felt a thrill run through her, a mix of excitement and fear. She'd never been anywhere like this, never felt so out of place and yet so alive.

As the night went on, Travis kept the drinks flowin', his eyes never leavin' hers. He leaned in close, his breath warm against her ear, his words soft and seductive. "I like you, Carmen," he whispered, his voice low and rough. "I like you a lot."

Carmen's heart fluttered, her cheeks flushin' with heat. She wanted to believe him, wanted to believe that he really cared, that he wasn't just playin' her like everyone said. But there was a part of her, a small, naggin' voice in the back of her mind, that couldn't shake the feelin' that maybe, just maybe, she was in over her head.

The next day, she couldn't concentrate at work. Her thoughts kept driftin' back to Travis, to the way he made her feel, like she was the only girl in the world. She tried to focus, tried to push him out of her mind, but it was no use. He was everywhere, in her thoughts, in her dreams, a constant presence that she couldn't escape.

That night, as she lay in bed, her phone buzzed with a new message. It was from Travis, of course. "Had a great time last night, beautiful. Can't stop thinkin' 'bout you. Can I see you again?"

Carmen stared at the screen, her heart poundin' in her chest. She knew she should say no, knew she should end it before things got too serious. But as she typed out her reply, her fingers movin' almost of their own accord, she couldn't help but feel a thrill of excitement, a rush of adrenaline that she hadn't felt in years.

"Sure," she typed back, her hands shakin' slightly. "I'd like that."

As she hit send, she couldn't shake the feelin' that she was standin' on the edge of somethin' big, somethin' dangerous. And as much as she tried to convince herself otherwise, she knew deep down that she was already in too deep.

She tossed and turned, tryin' to ignore the doubts, the worries that kept creepin' in. She wanted to believe that Travis was different, that he was the real deal. But in her heart, she couldn't help but wonder if maybe, just maybe, she was makin' a mistake.

But it was too late now. She was in it, and there was no turnin' back. And as she lay there, starin' up at the ceilin', she knew that things were about to get real complicated, real fast.

Chapter 4: A Taste of the High Life

Carmen didn't know what she was gettin' herself into when she let Travis into her world. At first, it was just little things—flowers, jewelry, and sweet words that made her feel special. But soon, Travis was takin' it to a whole new level, showin' her a life she ain't never seen before. It was like somethin' out of a movie, and Carmen found herself drawn into it, her head spinnin' from all the luxury and glamour he was throwin' her way.

One Friday night, Travis rolled up outside her apartment in a brand-new Range Rover, the sleek black paint shinin' under the streetlights. Carmen stood on the curb, her mouth hangin' open as she stared at the car. She ain't never seen nothin' like it, not in real life, anyway.

"Damn, Trav, where you get this?" she asked, her voice full of awe as she climbed into the passenger seat, her fingers brushin' over the leather interior.

Travis just grinned, his white teeth flashin' in the dim light. "You like it, baby? This ride's just the beginning. I'ma show you what livin' really look like."

Carmen laughed, her heart flutterin' with excitement. She wanted to ask him how he could afford a car like this, but she knew better than to question it. Travis had his ways, and she didn't wanna ruin the moment. So she just smiled, leanin' back in the seat as he revved the engine and sped off into the night.

He took her to a club downtown, the kinda place where the drinks cost more than her rent and the women dripped with diamonds and designer clothes. Carmen felt out of place, her simple dress and modest heels makin' her stand out among the glitter and glamour. But Travis didn't seem to care. He walked in like he owned the joint, his arm wrapped around Carmen's waist, guidin' her through the crowd.

They made their way to the VIP section, where a bottle of champagne waited for them on ice. Travis poured her a glass, his eyes never leavin' hers as he handed it to her. "To us," he said, clinkin' his glass against hers.

Carmen took a sip, the bubbles ticklin' her nose. She couldn't remember the last time she'd had champagne, if she ever had. It tasted like wealth, like a life she'd only ever dreamed of. And here she was, right in the middle of it, all because of Travis.

As the night wore on, Carmen found herself loosin' up, the champagne flowin' through her veins, makin' her feel light and carefree. Travis was right there beside her, his hands all over her, whisperin' sweet nothings in her ear. She knew she should be worried, that this wasn't the kinda life she was used to, but she couldn't help herself. Travis made her feel alive, like she was finally livin' instead of just existin'.

"Damn, Trav," she murmured as he pulled her close, his hands roamin' over her body. "This some crazy shit, you know that? I ain't never done nothin' like this before."

Travis chuckled, his breath warm against her neck. "Get used to it, baby. This just the start. I'm gonna take you places you ain't never been, show you things you ain't never seen. Just stick with me, and I'll make sure you live like a queen."

Carmen felt a shiver run down her spine, a mix of fear and excitement coursin' through her. She wanted to believe him, wanted to think that this could be her life, that she could have all this and more. But deep down, she knew it wasn't that simple. Nothin' ever was.

Still, she couldn't bring herself to pull away. Travis was like a drug, intoxicatin' and addictive, and she was hooked. She let him lead her through the night, drownin' in the sights and sounds of the city, forgettin' all about her worries and doubts.

Over the next few weeks, Travis continued to spoil her, takin' her on shoppin' sprees at the high-end boutiques downtown. Carmen couldn't believe her luck as she tried on dress after dress, each one more beautiful than the last. Travis would sit back and watch, his eyes dark with desire as he nodded in approval.

"That one, baby," he'd say, pointin' to a tight red dress that hugged her curves. "You lookin' fine as hell in that. We takin' it."

Carmen would blush, her heart racin' as she twirled in front of the mirror. She'd never had anyone treat her like this, never had a man who wanted to spoil her, make her feel like a princess. It was a heady feelin', and she found herself fallin' for Travis more and more each day.

But not everyone was so thrilled with her new lifestyle. Her mama, always suspicious, started to notice the changes. The new clothes, the late nights, the fancy jewelry. She pulled Carmen aside one night, her face etched with worry.

"Carmen, what's goin' on with you? You actin' different, and I don't like it. This Travis boy... he ain't good for you. I can see it in his eyes. You need to be careful, baby. This ain't you."

Carmen sighed, turnin' away from her mama's concerned gaze. "Mama, I'm fine. Travis, he's takin' care of me. He's showin' me a good time. I know what I'm doin'."

Her mama shook her head, her lips pressed into a thin line. "I just don't want you gettin' hurt, Carmen. You got so much goin' for you, and I don't want you throwin' it all away for some man who don't care 'bout nothin' but you or himself."

Carmen felt a pang of guilt, but she pushed it aside. She didn't wanna hear it, didn't wanna think about the consequences. She was havin' fun, livin' a life she'd never imagined, and she wasn't ready to give it up. Not yet.

Her friends were no better. They'd corner her at work, their eyes full of judgment and disapproval. "Girl, what you doin' messin' with Travis? He's trouble, Carmen. You know that. You gotta be careful."

But Carmen would just smile, brushin' off their concerns. "I got this, okay? Travis ain't as bad as y'all think. He's got a good heart. Y'all just don't see it."

And maybe they didn't. Maybe they were just jealous, couldn't understand what she saw in him. But Carmen did. She saw the way he looked at her, the way he made her feel. He was showin' her a world she'd only ever dreamed of, and she wasn't ready to let it go.

One night, Travis took her to a party in a penthouse suite downtown. The place was packed, the air thick with smoke and the sound of laughter and music. Carmen felt a thrill run through her as she walked in, Travis's hand on the small of her back, walkin' with her through the crowd.

They found a spot on the balcony, overlookin' the city below. Travis pulled her close, his arms wrapped around her waist, his lips brushin' against her ear. "You like this, baby?" he murmured, his voice low and seductive. "This what you been missin' out on."

Carmen nodded, her heart racin' as she looked out at the city lights, the skyline stretchin' out before her. "Yeah, Trav. This is... this is somethin' else."

Travis chuckled, his hands slidin' down her back. "Stick with me, Carmen. I'll make sure you never go without. I'll take care of you, make sure you livin' the life you deserve."

Carmen felt a shiver run down her spine, a mix of excitement and fear coursin' through her. She wanted to believe him, wanted to think that this could be her life, that she could have all this and more. But deep down, she knew it wasn't that simple. Nothin' ever was.

As the night wore on, Carmen found herself loosin' track of time, the hours slippin' away in a blur of music and laughter. Travis was right there beside her, his hands all over her, whisperin' sweet nothings in her ear.

But as the night wore on and the alcohol flowed, Carmen started to see a different side of Travis. He was more aggressive, more possessive, his hands grippin' her too tight, his words slurrin' as he talked about his "business." She tried to ignore it, to focus on the good, but it was hard. Harder than she thought it would be.

At one point, she saw him pullin' a guy aside, his voice low and angry. She couldn't hear what he was sayin', but she could see the tension in his body, the way his fists clenched at his sides. She felt a sense of unease, a nigglin' doubt in the back of her mind.

Chapter 5: The First Betrayal

The rumors hit Carmen like a punch to the gut, leaving her breathless and reeling. She was at the salon, gettin' her hair done, when she heard the whispers. Two girls were talkin' loud enough for everyone to hear, not even botherin' to keep their voices down. They were gossipy, full of that mean kinda laughter that made Carmen's skin crawl.

"Girl, did you see Travis at the club last night?" one of them said, her voice dripping with satisfaction. "He was all up on some girl, all hugged up and kissin' on her like he ain't got no damn sense."

Carmen's heart stopped. She felt her stomach twistin', her hands clenchin' into fists on her lap. She tried to keep her face straight, pretendin' she wasn't listenin', but her mind was spinnin' out of control.

"Yeah, I saw 'em too," the other one chimed in. "That nigga ain't shit. Playin' games with everybody. He supposed to be with some other girl. She better wake up and see what's goin' on 'fore she get hurt."

Carmen's breath hitched, a hot tear slidin' down her cheek. She didn't wanna believe it, didn't wanna think that Travis could do somethin' like this to her. But the seed of doubt had been planted, and it was growin' like a weed, takin' root in her chest, chokin' her with fear.

She left the salon without sayin' a word, her heart poundin' in her ears, drownin' out the sound of the city around her. She needed to talk to Travis, needed to hear him tell her it wasn't true, that it was all just a misunderstanding. But deep down, she knew. She knew somethin' wasn't right.

When she got to his place, she found him loungin' on the couch, a blunt hangin' from his lips, his eyes half-closed in a lazy haze. He looked up when she came in, his expression shiftin' to surprise when he saw her face.

"Yo, Carmen, what's good?" he said, sittin' up, his eyes narrowin' as he took in her tear-streaked cheeks and red-rimmed eyes. "What's wrong, baby?"

Carmen crossed her arms over her chest, tryin' to hold herself together. "I heard somethin' today, Travis," she said, her voice tight with emotion. "People sayin' you was at the club last night with another woman. Kissin' on her, actin' like you single."

Travis's face hardened, his eyes turnin' cold as he leaned back, takin' a long drag from the blunt before blowin' the smoke out slow. "That's bullshit, Carmen. You know how people talk. Always tryin' to start some shit, tryin' to get in everybody business."

Carmen shook her head, her hands tremblin' at her sides. "It wasn't just one person, Travis. It was a bunch of them. I need to know the truth. Did you do it?"

Travis sighed, droppin' the blunt in an ashtray, rubbin' his face with his hands. "Man, I ain't got time for this. Yeah, I was at the club, but I wasn't doin' nothin'. Just hangin' out, havin' a good time. You know how it is."

Carmen felt her heart breakin', the pieces shatterin' in her chest. She wanted to believe him, wanted to trust that he was tellin' her the truth. But the doubt was there, lurkin' in the back of her mind, eatin' away at her.

"Please, Travis," she whispered, her voice barely audible over the sound of her own heartbeat. "Just tell me the truth. I can't take this."

Travis stood up, crossin' the room in a few long strides, pullin' her into his arms, his hands rough and calloused against her skin. "Baby, you gotta believe me," he murmured, his voice low and urgent. "I ain't messin' around on you. You the only one I want, the only one I need. I swear."

Carmen felt the tears spillin' over, her body shakin' with silent sobs. She wanted to push him away, to run out the door and never look back. But she couldn't. She was trapped, caught in his web, unable to break free.

Travis held her tight, his hands movin' up to cup her face, forcin' her to look at him. "Listen to me, Carmen. I'm sorry, a'ight? If I made you feel like I wasn't committed, if I did somethin' to hurt you, I'm sorry. But you gotta trust me. I ain't goin' nowhere."

He reached into his pocket, pullin' out a small velvet box, poppin' it open to reveal a delicate gold necklace, a heart-shaped pendant danglin' from a thin chain. "I got this for you," he said, his voice soft, almost tender. "To show you how much you mean to me. You my girl, Carmen. Ain't nobody else."

Carmen stared at the necklace, her breath catchin' in her throat. It was beautiful, the kinda thing she'd never be able to afford on her own. She wanted to believe him, wanted to think that he really did care, that this was just a one-time thing. She reached out, takin' the necklace, her fingers brushin' against his as she did.

"Thank you," she whispered, her voice choked with emotion. "I just... I need you to be honest with me, Travis. I can't do this if I don't trust you."

Travis nodded, pullin' her into a kiss, his lips hot and demandin' against hers. "I'mma be better, baby. I promise. Just give me another chance."

Carmen closed her eyes, lettin' herself get lost in the feel of his lips, his hands, his words. She wanted to believe him, wanted to think that things could go back to how they were. But there was a part of her, deep down, that couldn't shake the feelin' that this was just the beginning of somethin' much worse.

Over the next few days, Carmen tried to put the incident behind her, tellin' herself that it was just a misunderstanding, that Travis wouldn't do somethin' like that again. But the doubt was still there, lingerin' like a shadow, always at the back of her mind.

She started to notice things, little things that didn't add up. Late-night calls that he wouldn't answer in front of her, conversations that would stop when she walked into the room. He'd disappear for hours at a time, leavin' her alone and wonderin' where he was, what he was doin'.

But every time she tried to bring it up, to ask him what was goin' on, he'd brush her off, tellin' her she was imaginin' things, that she needed to relax and trust him. And Carmen, not wantin' to push him away, would nod and let it go, tellin' herself that she was bein' paranoid, that she needed to stop worryin' so much.

But the unease never went away. It was always there, a constant presence, a gnawin' ache in her chest that wouldn't let her rest. She tried to focus on her work, on her studies, but it was hard. Her mind was always driftin' back to Travis, to the doubt, the fear, the pain.

One night, as she lay in bed, she heard his phone buzzin' on the nightstand. She glanced over, seein' the screen light up with a name she didn't recognize. Her heart skipped a beat, her hands clenchin' the sheets as she watched him reach over, grab the phone, and turn it face down without answerin' it.

"Who was that?" she asked, her voice tight, her eyes fixed on him.

Travis didn't look at her, his expression unreadable. "Nobody important," he said, his tone dismissive. "Just some business shit. Go back to sleep, baby."

Carmen nodded, her mind racin' with questions she didn't dare ask. She wanted to believe him, wanted to think that everything was okay, that she was just imaginin' things. But the doubt was there, stronger than ever, gnawin' at her, refusin' to let her rest.

As she closed her eyes, tryin' to will herself to sleep, she couldn't shake the feelin' that things were spiralin' out of control, that she was losin' herself in Travis's world, a world she wasn't sure she wanted to be a part of.

But it was too late to turn back now. She was in too deep, and she didn't know how to get out. And as she drifted off, her dreams haunted by shadows and whispers, she knew that things were only gonna get worse from here.

Chapter 6: Rumors and Confrontations

Carmen stepped into the beauty salon, the familiar hum of blow dryers and chatter filling the air. It was a small, cramped space, but it was the go-to spot in the neighborhood for anyone lookin' to get their hair laid or nails done. Carmen liked it there; it was one of the few places she could unwind and forget about the stress of work and school.

She was sittin' in the chair, flippin' through a magazine, tryin' to push the thoughts of Travis and his late-night phone calls outta her mind. The doubts had been eatin' away at her, but she couldn't bring herself to confront him again. She didn't wanna believe he was out there messin' around. She didn't wanna think about what that meant for them.

As she was gettin' her nails done, Carmen heard the front door open and the sound of high heels clickin' against the linoleum floor. She glanced up, seein' a tall woman with long, wavy hair and a tight dress that showed off every curve. She was beautiful, the kinda girl who turned heads wherever she went.

The woman walked straight up to Carmen, her eyes narrowin' as she looked her up and down. "You Carmen?" she demanded, her voice loud and accusatory.

Carmen blinked, startled by the sudden confrontation. "Yeah, I'm Carmen," she said, her voice uncertain. "Who are you?"

The woman's lips curled into a sneer. "I'm Tasha. Travis's girl. And you? You need to back the fuck off."

Carmen's heart stopped. She felt like the floor had just dropped out from under her. She stared at Tasha, her mind strugglin' to process what she was hearin'. "Travis's girl?" she repeated, her voice barely a whisper. "What are you talkin' about?"

Tasha laughed, a harsh, ugly sound. "Don't act all innocent, bitch. I know you been fuckin' around with him. I seen the messages, seen the pics. He's been playin' both of us, and I'm here to set the record straight."

The room went silent. Everyone in the salon was watchin' now, their eyes wide, their mouths hangin' open in shock. Carmen felt her face burnin' with embarrassment, her hands shakin' in her lap. She didn't know what to say, didn't know how to defend herself. She'd never been in a situation like this before.

"Tasha, I…I didn't know," Carmen stammered, her voice breakin'. "I thought I was the only one. I swear, I didn't know."

Tasha's eyes flashed with anger. "Bullshit. You knew damn well what you was doin'. You think you special or somethin'? Think you the only one he be takin' out, buyin' shit for? You just another dumb bitch fallin' for his lies."

Carmen felt tears prickin' at the corners of her eyes. She wanted to yell back, to defend herself, but the words wouldn't come. She was too humiliated, too hurt. She couldn't believe this was happenin'. She couldn't believe Travis had been playin' her like this.

"Tasha, please," she whispered, her voice barely audible. "I didn't know. I'm sorry."

But Tasha wasn't hearin' it. She stepped closer, her hand raisin' up like she was about to slap Carmen across the face. "You ain't sorry yet, bitch," she yelled. "But you gonna be."

Carmen flinched, closin' her eyes, waitin' for the blow. But it never came. One of the stylists stepped in, grabbin' Tasha's arm and pullin' her back. "Aight, that's enough, Tasha," she said firmly. "Take that shit outside. This ain't the place."

Tasha yanked her arm away, glarin' at Carmen one last time before turnin' on her heel and stormin' outta the salon, her heels clickin' angrily against the floor. The door slammed shut behind her, and the room fell into a tense, uncomfortable silence.

Carmen sat there, her hands coverin' her face, her whole body shakin' with sobs. She couldn't believe this was happenin'. She couldn't believe she'd been so stupid, so naive. She'd let Travis play her like a damn fool, and now everyone knew it.

The stylist next to her, a woman named Keisha, reached out, puttin' a hand on her shoulder. "Hey, Carmen, you okay, girl?" she asked softly, her voice filled with concern.

Carmen nodded, even though she wasn't okay. She wasn't even close to okay. She felt like her world was fallin' apart, like everything she thought she knew was a lie. She didn't know what to do, didn't know how to fix this.

"I'm sorry," she mumbled, wipin' at her eyes. "I'm so sorry."

Keisha gave her a sympathetic smile. "Ain't nothin' for you to be sorry about, girl. You ain't the one who did wrong here. Travis did. He's the one playin' games, not you."

Carmen nodded, but the words didn't make her feel any better. She still felt humiliated, still felt like a fool. She didn't know how she was gonna face anyone after this.

After a few minutes, she managed to pull herself together enough to pay and leave. She walked outta the salon, her head down, her heart heavy with shame. She didn't know where she was goin', didn't know what she was gonna do. She just knew she needed to get away, needed to be alone.

She ended up at her friend Mariah's house, knockin' on the door with tears still streamin' down her face. Mariah opened the door, her eyes goin' wide when she saw the state Carmen was in.

"Girl, what the hell happened?" Mariah demanded, pullin' Carmen inside and closin' the door behind her. "You look like you just seen a ghost."

Carmen broke down, sobbin' uncontrollably as she tried to explain what had happened at the salon, the confrontation with Tasha, the humiliation, the pain. Mariah listened, her face growin' more and more angry with every word.

"That motherfucker!!," she yelled when Carmen finished, her hands clenchin' into fists at her sides. "I knew he was no good. I told you, Carmen. I told you he was trouble. And now look what he done to you."

Carmen shook her head, her tears still flowin'. "I know, Mariah. I know. I shoulda listened. I shoulda known better."

Mariah sighed, pullin' Carmen into a tight hug. "It ain't your fault, Carmen. You just wanted to believe the best in him, and he took advantage of that. But you gotta let him go, girl. He ain't worth all this pain."

Carmen nodded, but she wasn't sure she could do it. She still loved Travis, still wanted to believe that he could change, that he could be the man she needed him to be. But after what happened today, she didn't know if she could keep foolin' herself.

Later that night, Carmen sat on Mariah's couch, starin' at her phone, her fingers hoverin' over Travis's name. She wanted to call him, to hear his voice, to ask him why he'd done this to her. But she was scared, scared of what he might say, scared of the truth.

Mariah sat down next to her, her expression serious. "Carmen, you gotta make a decision," she said firmly. "You either let him go, or you gonna keep lettin' him walk all over you. But you can't keep doin' this to yourself. It ain't healthy."

Carmen nodded, her heart heavy with indecision. She knew Mariah was right. She knew she needed to let Travis go, needed to move on with her life. But she didn't know how. She didn't know if she was strong enough.

"I just...I don't know if I can," she whispered, her voice breakin'. "I love him, Mariah. I know it sounds crazy, but I do."

Mariah sighed, shakin' her head. "Love don't mean shit if it's breakin' you, Carmen. You deserve better than this. You deserve someone who's gonna treat you right, who's gonna respect you. Not someone who's out here playin' games and hurtin' you."

Carmen nodded, tears fillin' her eyes once again. She knew Mariah was right. She knew she needed to be strong, needed to walk away. But it was hard. Harder than she ever thought it would be.

As she sat there, starin' at her phone, she felt a wave of anger and sadness crash over her, leavin' her breathless. She didn't know what the future held, didn't know what she was gonna do. But she knew one thing for sure: she couldn't keep livin' like this. She couldn't keep lettin' Travis break her heart, over and over again.

And as she finally set the phone down, her hands shakin', she made a silent vow to herself. She was gonna find a way to move on. She was gonna find a way to be strong. Because she deserved better. She deserved more.

Chapter 7: The Apology Tour

Carmen was sittin' on her bed, starin' at the wall when she heard the knock on her door. It was a soft knock, hesitant, almost like whoever was on the other side wasn't sure if they should be there. She didn't need to guess who it was. She knew. Deep down, she knew. Her heart sank into her stomach, a mix of anger and sorrow swellin' inside her chest.

She wiped her eyes, takin' a deep breath as she got up and walked to the door. When she opened it, there he was, standin' there like he ain't had a care in the world, holdin' a bouquet of roses in one hand and a box of chocolates in the other.

"Carmen, baby, please, just hear me out," Travis said, his voice low and full of desperation. His eyes were soft, full of regret, and for a moment, Carmen felt her resolve start to crumble.

But then she remembered Tasha, the way she had looked at her in the salon, the way everyone had stared, whisperin', laughin'. Her anger flared up again, stronger than before, and she glared at him, her jaw clenchin'.

"What you want, Travis?" she snapped, her voice cold. "You think flowers and some damn chocolates gon' fix what you did? You think that's all it takes?"

Travis flinched, like her words had slapped him in the face. He stepped forward, tryin' to hand her the flowers, but she just folded her arms over her chest, refusin' to take them.

"Look, I know I fucked up," he admitted, his voice tight with emotion. "I know I hurt you, Carmen. But I swear, I didn't mean to. I just... I got caught up, you know? This life, it's all I know. It's hard, tryin' to be different."

Carmen scoffed, rollin' her eyes. "Oh, so now it's the life's fault, huh? Now it's everybody else's fault but yours?"

Travis shook his head, his shoulders slumpin'. "No, no, I ain't sayin' that. I know it's on me. I just... I grew up in this shit, Carmen. Ain't nobody ever taught me how to love right. My pops, he was the same way, runnin' 'round on my moms, playin' her. I guess I just... I don't know any better."

Carmen felt a pang of sympathy tug at her heart. She knew Travis's upbringing hadn't been easy. She knew about his pops, the way he used to beat on his moms, the way he'd left when Travis was just a kid. She'd heard the stories, seen the pain in Travis's eyes when he talked about it. And as much as she wanted to stay mad, she couldn't help but feel sorry for him.

But she wasn't ready to let him off the hook just yet. "That's a sorry-ass excuse, Travis," she said, her voice firm. "You a grown-ass man. You know right from wrong. You chose to do this. You chose to hurt me."

Travis nodded, his face fallin'. "I know, I know. And I'm sorry, baby. I'm so sorry. I just... I don't wanna lose you, Carmen. I don't wanna lose the only good thing I got in my life. Please, just give me another chance. I'll do better. I promise."

Carmen stared at him, her heart achin'. She wanted to believe him, wanted to think that maybe, just maybe, he was tellin' the truth. She wanted to believe that he could change, that he could be the man she needed him to be. But she'd been down this road before, and she knew how it ended.

Still, she couldn't bring herself to close the door. She couldn't bring herself to walk away. "Why should I trust you?" she asked, her voice barely a whisper. "Why should I believe anything you say?"

Travis stepped closer, his eyes never leavin' hers. "Because I love you, Carmen," he said softly. "I love you more than anything. And I'm willin' to do whatever it takes to prove it. I'll quit the streets, I'll get a real job. Hell, I'll even go to therapy if that's what you want. Just... please, don't leave me."

Carmen felt her resolve weakenin', her heart breakin' all over again. She wanted to believe him. She wanted to believe that he could change, that he could be the man she deserved. And maybe, just maybe, he was tellin' the truth. Maybe he really was willin' to change.

She took a deep breath, her mind racin'. "Okay," she said finally, her voice shakin'. "Okay, Travis. I'll give you another chance. But this is it. This is your last chance. If you fuck up again, I'm done. You hear me? I'm done."

Travis's face lit up with relief, and he reached out, pullin' her into a tight hug. "Thank you, baby. Thank you. I swear, you won't regret this. I'm gonna make it right. I'm gonna make us right."

Carmen nodded, her arms wrappin' around him, holdin' him close. She wanted to believe him. She wanted to believe that they could have a future together, that she could save him from the streets, from himself.

Over the next few weeks, Travis was a different man. He was attentive, thoughtful, always there when she needed him. He'd show up at her job with lunch, takin' her out on her breaks, makin' her laugh like he used to. He'd take her out to nice dinners, buy her gifts, shower her with affection.

Carmen felt herself fallin' for him all over again, her heart swellin' with hope. She started to dream of a future together, of a life away from the streets, away from all the pain and drama. She dreamed of a life where they could be happy, where they could build somethin' real.

But deep down, she knew it wasn't gonna be easy. She knew Travis had a lot of demons to face, a lot of baggage to unpack. But she was willin' to stand by him, to help him through it. She believed in him. She believed in their love.

One night, they were sittin' on her couch, watchin' a movie, when Travis turned to her, his expression serious. "Carmen, I been thinkin'," he said quietly. "I wanna get out. I wanna leave the streets behind, for real this time. I wanna be a better man, for you, for us."

Carmen's heart skipped a beat, her eyes fillin' with tears. "You mean that?" she asked, her voice tremblin'.

Travis nodded, takin' her hand in his. "Yeah, I mean it. I'm done with all that shit. I wanna be with you, Carmen. I wanna build a life with you. A real life."

Carmen felt a sob rise in her throat, and she threw her arms around him, buryin' her face in his shoulder. "I love you, Travis," she whispered, her voice muffled by his shirt. "I love you so much."

"I love you too, baby," Travis murmured, kissin' the top of her head. "And I'm gonna prove it to you. I'm gonna be the man you deserve."

For a moment, Carmen allowed herself to believe it. She allowed herself to believe that they could have a future, that Travis could change, that their love was strong enough to overcome any obstacle.

But as the days went by, the doubts started to creep back in. She'd catch Travis on the phone, speakin' in hushed tones, his face tense and serious. He'd disappear for hours, leavin' her wonderin' where he was, what he was doin'.

And then there were the rumors. She'd hear people talkin' on the street, whisperin' about Travis, about the deals he was still makin', the people he was still runnin' with. She tried to ignore it, tried to push it outta her mind, but it was hard. Harder than she thought it would be.

One night, as she lay in bed next to him, listenin' to his steady breathin', she couldn't shake the feelin' that somethin' was off. She wanted to believe in him, wanted to believe in their love, but the doubt was there, naggin' at her, eatin' away at her.

And as she closed her eyes, tryin' to will herself to sleep, she couldn't shake the feelin', that their love was a fragile thing, teeterin' on the brink of collapse. She didn't know what the future held, didn't know if they could make it, but she knew one thing for sure: she was in too deep to turn back now. And as much as she wanted to, she couldn't walk away. Not yet. Not when there was still a glimmer of hope, a chance that things could be different. That they could be different.

Chapter 8: Deepening the Bond

Travis had a way of makin' Carmen forget all the bad shit. Whenever things got tense or ugly, he'd swoop in, talkin' sweet and takin' her mind off everything. He started takin' her outta town, showin' her places she ain't never seen, like he was tryin' to prove somethin'. It was like he was showin' her a different side of him, somethin' softer, somethin' better than what she saw in the streets.

One weekend, Travis surprised her with a trip to the coast. They left late Friday night, drivin' in his car, the bass bumpin' loud, his hand restin' on her thigh. They rode with the windows down, the wind blowin' through her hair, the city lights disappearin' behind 'em. Carmen looked out the window, watchin' the world blur by, feelin' free in a way she never had before.

"Ain't nobody got what we got, baby," Travis said, his voice low and smooth. "They can't stand to see us happy. That's why they talkin'. That's why they hatin'."

Carmen nodded, a small smile playin' on her lips. She wanted to believe him, wanted to think that what they had was special, that it was somethin' worth fightin' for. "I know, Trav. I just hate how they look at me, like I'm doin' somethin' wrong. Like I'm crazy for lovin' you."

Travis chuckled, shakin' his head. "Fuck 'em. They don't know shit. They don't know what we got. All they know is their own misery, tryin' to bring us down to their level. But we ain't got time for that, a'ight? We got each other, and that's all that matters."

Carmen leaned over, kissin' him on the cheek, her hand slippin' into his. She wanted to believe it, wanted to drown out the doubts and the whispers. She knew people were talkin', knew they were judgin' her for bein' with him. But she didn't care. Not when she was with Travis, not when he was lookin' at her like she was the only girl in the world.

They spent the weekend at a fancy beach resort, the kinda place Carmen never thought she'd see, let alone stay in. Travis had booked a suite, the room overlookin' the ocean, the sound of the waves crashin' against the shore lulling her to sleep at night. It was paradise, somethin' out of a dream, and Carmen couldn't get enough of it.

They spent their days loungin' on the beach, swimmin' in the crystal-clear water, and eatin' at high-end restaurants where the waiters wore bow ties and the food was served on silver platters. Travis was always smilin', always tellin' her how much he loved her, how much he wanted to spend the rest of his life with her.

One night, as they were sittin' on the balcony, watchin' the sun dip below the horizon, Travis turned to her, his eyes serious. "I been thinkin' 'bout us, Carmen," he said quietly, his hand squeezin' hers. "I wanna build somethin' real with you. I wanna get out the game, for good. Start fresh, just me and you."

Carmen's heart skipped a beat, her eyes fillin' with tears. She wanted to believe him, wanted to think that they could have a future together, away from the streets, away from all the pain and drama. "You mean that, Travis? You really wanna get out?"

Travis nodded, his expression earnest. "Yeah, I mean it. I'm tired of this life, tired of lookin' over my shoulder, wonderin' who's gonna try and take me down next. I just wanna be with you, Carmen. I wanna give you the life you deserve."

Carmen felt a sob rise in her throat, and she threw her arms around him, buryin' her face in his shoulder. "I love you, Travis," she whispered, her voice muffled by his shirt. "I love you so much."

"I love you too, baby," Travis murmured, kissin' the top of her head. "And I'm gonna prove it to you. I'm gonna be the man you want."

For a moment, Carmen allowed herself to believe it. She allowed herself to believe that they could have a future, that Travis could change, that their love was strong enough to overcome any obstacle. But deep down, she knew it wasn't gonna be easy. She knew Travis had a lot of shit to face, a lot of baggage to unpack and heal. But she was willin' to stand by him, to help him through it. She believed in him. She believed in their love.

When they got back to the city, Carmen noticed that things had started to change. People were talkin' more, whisperin' behind her back, givin' her those side-eye glances whenever she walked by. She could feel their judgment, their disapproval, but she tried to ignore it. She told herself they were just jealous, that they couldn't stand to see her happy, to see her livin' a life they could only dream of.

But it wasn't just strangers who were talkin'. Her friends had started to notice the change in her too. Mariah pulled her aside one day, her face full of concern. "Carmen, what's goin' on with you, girl? You actin' different, dressin' all flashy, missin' classes. This ain't like you."

Carmen shrugged, tryin' to play it off. "I'm fine, Mariah. I'm just... I'm happy, okay? Travis makes me happy."

Mariah frowned, shakin' her head. "Happy? Girl, you don't look happy. You look lost. You lettin' him change you, Carmen. And not for the better."

Carmen felt anger flare up inside her. She was tired of everyone judgin' her, tired of everyone actin' like they knew what was best for her. "I ain't lost, Mariah. I know exactly what I'm doin'. And Travis, he's tryin' to change. He's tryin' to be better."

Mariah sighed, her expression softenin'. "I just don't wanna see you get hurt, Carmen. You deserve better than this. You deserve better than him."

Carmen shook her head, turnin' away. "You don't know him like I do, Mariah. You don't see the good in him. All you see is the streets, but there's more to him than that. I just wish you'd understand."

Mariah watched her go, her eyes filled with sadness. Carmen could feel her gaze on her back as she walked away, but she didn't look back. She couldn't. She didn't wanna see the disappointment, didn't wanna see the doubt. She wanted to believe in Travis, wanted to believe in their future.

As the days went by, Carmen found herself withdrawin' more and more. She started skippin' classes, makin' excuses to her professors, tellin' herself she'd make it up later. She stopped hangin' out with her friends, avoidin' their calls, their texts, knowin' they'd just try to talk her outta seein' Travis.

But no matter how hard she tried to ignore the whispers, they were always there, lingerin' in the back of her mind, gnawin' at her like a hungry dog. She knew people were talkin', knew they were judgin' her, but she couldn't bring herself to care. She was in too deep, too far gone to turn back now.

One night, as she was walkin' home from the store, she heard someone call her name. She turned around, seein' a group of girls from the neighborhood standin' on the corner, their arms crossed over their chests, their eyes narrowin' as they looked her up and down.

"Look at you, Carmen," one of them sneered, her voice full of contempt. "Thinkin' you better than us now, huh? Ridin' 'round in that fancy cars, wearin' those expensive clothes. You just another dumb bitch fallin' for an aint shit nigga."

Carmen felt her cheeks burnin' with anger, but she kept her head high, refusin' to let them see how much their words hurt. "Y'all just jealous," she shot back, her voice steady. "Y'all wish you had what I got. But you don't, and you never will."

The girls laughed, shakin' their heads. "Jealous? Of you? Please. We ain't jealous of no girl who's dumb enough to think she can change a man like Travis. He's gonna break your heart, Carmen. Just like he's done to every other girl before you."

Carmen felt a lump form in her throat, but she swallowed it down, refusin' to let them see her cry. She turned on her heel, walkin' away, her hands clenchin' into fists at her sides. She didn't wanna believe them, didn't wanna think that they might be right. But their words stayed with her, echoing in her mind, haunting her every step.

As she lay in bed that night, starin' up at the ceilin', she couldn't shake the feelin' that things were spiralin' out of control. She wanted to believe in Travis, wanted to believe in their love, but the doubt was there, always there, lurkin' in the shadows, waitin' to pounce.

And as she closed her eyes, tryin' to drown out the noise, she knew one thing for sure: she was standin' on the edge, and she didn't know if she'd be able to pull herself back. Not this time. Not with Travis.

Chapter 9: Dark Realities

Carmen had always known there was a dark side to Travis, but she had never seen it up close. Not like this. She'd heard the whispers, the rumors about what he did, but she'd pushed them to the back of her mind, convincing herself that it was just talk. Now, she was starting to see the truth with her own eyes, and it scared her more than she wanted to admit.

It started one night when Travis took her to a run-down warehouse on the edge of town. The place was sketchy as hell, the kind of spot you didn't wanna be caught in after dark. The windows were boarded up, the walls covered in graffiti, and the whole place smelled like piss and stale beer. Carmen could hear the sound of distant sirens, the hum of the city in the background, a reminder that they were never too far from trouble.

"Trav, what we doin' here?" Carmen asked, her voice tight with nerves as she followed him through the maze of crates and old machinery.

Travis didn't answer right away. He just kept walkin', his eyes focused straight ahead, his jaw clenched. Finally, he stopped in front of a group of men, all of them dressed in dark clothes, their faces hard and unwelcomin'. Carmen recognized a few of them from around the neighborhood—guys with bad reputations, known for dealin' and other shady shit.

"Stay close to me, a'ight?" Travis muttered, his voice low. He gave her a quick glance, his expression unreadable. "And don't say nothin'. Just keep quiet and let me handle this."

Carmen nodded, her heart poundin' in her chest. She didn't like this. Not one bit. But she trusted Travis, believed he knew what he was doin'. She stayed behind him, her eyes wide as she watched the scene unfold.

One of the men stepped forward, a sneer on his lips. "Yo, Travis, you got the stuff?" he asked, his voice rough and filled with suspicion.

Travis nodded, reachin' into his jacket and pullin' out a small package wrapped in plastic. "Yeah, I got it," he said coolly, tossin' it to the guy. "Now, where's my money?"

The man caught the package, inspectin' it for a moment before noddin' to another guy behind him. That guy stepped forward, handin' Travis a thick wad of cash. Carmen's stomach twisted as she watched. She knew what this was. She knew what was goin' down. She wasn't stupid. But seein' it, bein' a part of it, was a whole different story.

Travis took the money, countin' it quickly before stuffin' it into his pocket. "We good?" he asked, his tone calm, almost bored.

The man nodded, but his eyes were still hard, his gaze shiftin' to Carmen. "Who's the girl?" he asked, his voice laced with curiosity and something darker.

Travis stiffened, his body goin' rigid. "She's with me," he said sharply. "Don't worry about her. She ain't none of your concern."

The man smirked, his eyes lingerin' on Carmen for a beat too long. "Aight, man, whatever you say. Just makin' sure you ain't bringin' no trouble our way."

Travis didn't respond. He just grabbed Carmen's hand, pullin' her away, back toward the car. Carmen followed, her mind racin', her heart poundin' in her chest. She didn't know what to say, didn't know how to feel. She was scared, confused, but most of all, she was worried about Travis. She could see the tension in his shoulders, the anger simmerin' beneath the surface.

They drove in silence for a while, the city lights blurrin' past the windows. Carmen wanted to say somethin', wanted to ask him what the hell had just happened, but she didn't know where to start. She didn't want to make things worse.

Finally, Travis broke the silence, his voice tight and controlled. "I told you to stay outta my business, Carmen. Why you gotta come out tonight?"

Carmen bit her lip, her hands clenchin' in her lap. "I just wanted to be with you, Travis. I didn't know... I didn't know it was gonna be like that."

Travis sighed, shakin' his head. "This is my life, Carmen. This is what I do. I ain't proud of it, but it's what I gotta do to survive. You need to understand that."

Carmen nodded, her throat tight. She did understand. She knew the streets were rough, knew that people did what they had to do to get by. But this... this was somethin' else. She couldn't shake the image of those men, the way they'd looked at her, the way they'd talked to Travis. It was dangerous, and she knew it.

A few days later, Carmen found herself in another situation she wasn't prepared for. She was at Travis's place, chillin' on the couch while he handled some business in the other room. She could hear the muffled voices, the sound of a heated argument. She tried to ignore it, focusin' on the TV, but then she heard somethin' that made her blood run cold.

A loud crash, followed by shoutin', and then the unmistakable sound of flesh hittin' flesh. Carmen jumped up, her heart poundin' in her chest as she rushed to the doorway. She peeked inside, her eyes widenin' at the sight before her.

Travis was standin' over a guy, his fist clenched, blood drippin' from his knuckles. The guy was on the floor, his face a mess of blood and bruises, his body twitchin' in pain. Travis's face was twisted with rage, his chest heavin' as he glared down at the man.

"What the fuck did I tell you, huh?" Travis snarled, his voice low and dangerous. "I told you to keep your mouth shut, but you ain't listen. Now look at you. You just had to go and run your damn mouth, didn't you?"

The man groaned, spittin' out a mouthful of blood. "I'm sorry, man," he croaked, his voice weak. "I ain't mean to... I was just... I'm sorry."

Travis raised his fist again, ready to strike, but then he saw Carmen standin' in the doorway, her eyes wide with shock. He froze, his expression shiftin' from anger to somethin' else—somethin' like guilt.

"Carmen, get outta here," he said roughly, lowerin' his hand. "You shouldn't be seein' this."

Carmen couldn't move. She was rooted to the spot, her mind spinnin'. She knew Travis was capable of violence, knew he had a temper, but seein' it firsthand, seein' the blood on his hands, was a whole different story.

"Travis, what... what are you doin'?" she stammered, her voice barely a whisper. "Why... why are you doin' this?"

Travis wiped his face, his face a mask of frustration. "This is the game. This is how it is. You don't understand."

Carmen shook her head, her eyes fillin' with tears. "But you said... you said you wanted to get out, that you wanted to be different."

"I do!" Travis shouted, his voice crackin'. "I do wanna get out. But it ain't that easy. It ain't just somethin' you can walk away from. This life, it's got a hold on me, on all of us. And sometimes, you gotta do things you don't wanna do. You gotta make sacrifices."

Carmen felt a tear roll down her cheek, but she quickly wiped it away, tryin' to stay strong. She wanted to help him, wanted to be there for him, but she didn't know how. She didn't know if she could.

"Travis, I don't wanna see you like this," she said softly, her voice tremblin'. "I don't wanna see you hurtin' people, makin' deals with those kinds of men. It scares me."

Travis's face softened, and he took a step toward her, reachin' out to cup her cheek. "I know, baby. I know it scares you. But I'm tryin'. I'm tryin' to be better, for you, for us. You just gotta give me time."

Carmen nodded, but deep down, she wasn't sure how much more time she could give him. She was scared, more scared than she'd ever been in her life. She wanted to believe in him, wanted to believe that he could change, but the more she saw, the harder it was to hold on to that hope.

Over the next few weeks, things only got worse. Carmen started to see more and more of Travis's world—the drug deals, the shady characters, the violent altercations. She saw the way he handled his business, the way he talked to people, the way he used his fists to solve problems. It was ugly, and it was dangerous, and it was nothin' like the life she wanted for herself.

But she couldn't pull away. She couldn't bring herself to leave him.

Chapter 10: The Breaking Point

Carmen had a bad feelin' all day, somethin' in her gut didn't feel right. She tried to shake it off, tried to focus on work, on her classes, on anything but that damn naggin' in the back of her mind. But it wouldn't go away. It was like a shadow followin' her, whisperin' in her ear, tellin' her somethin' wasn't right.

She decided to go to Travis's place, hopin' seein' him would calm her nerves. Maybe they could talk, maybe they could finally figure things out. She was tired of the secrets, tired of the lies, tired of wonderin' where he was, what he was doin'. She needed answers, needed to know where they stood.

When she got to his apartment, she noticed the door was slightly ajar. Her heart skipped a beat, a chill runnin' down her spine. She pushed the door open, steppin' inside quietly, her eyes dartin' around the dimly lit room. The place was a mess—clothes scattered on the floor, empty bottles on the coffee table, the faint smell of weed hangin' in the air. She called out his name, her voice barely a whisper, but there was no answer.

As she made her way down the hallway, she heard it—a soft moan, comin' from the bedroom. Her heart pounded in her chest, her palms slick with sweat. She knew what she was about to see, but she couldn't stop herself. She pushed open the bedroom door, her breath catchin' in her throat at the sight in front of her.

There he was, Travis, layin' in bed with another woman. The girl was draped over him, her hair a wild mess, her eyes half-closed, her lips curled in a lazy smile. Carmen felt her world crumble around her, her heart shatterin' into a million pieces. She couldn't breathe, couldn't think. She just stood there, frozen, watchin' the man she loved betray her in the worst way possible.

"What the fuck is this?" Carmen finally choked out, her voice breakin', tears streamin' down her face.

Travis looked up, his eyes widenin' in shock, his face pale. "Carmen, I... I can explain," he stammered, pushin' the girl off him, scramblin' to cover himself.

"Explain?" Carmen spat, her voice risin', her hands shakin'. "Explain what, Travis? How you been lyin' to me this whole time? How you been fuckin' around behind my back? You think I'm stupid?"

The girl in the bed rolled her eyes, sittin' up and reachin' for her clothes. "Damn, I didn't know you had a girl," she muttered, glancin' between Carmen and Travis, a smug grin on her face. "Guess the joke's on me, huh?"

"Get the fuck out!" Carmen screamed, her voice crackin', her chest heavin' with sobs. "Get the fuck outttttt!"

Travis tried to reach for her, his face twisted with regret, but she slapped his hand away, her eyes blazin' with fury. "Don't touch me! Don't you fuckin' touch me!"

The girl grabbed her clothes, scurryin' out of the room, mumblin' under her breath. Travis stood there, lookin' like a deer caught in headlights, his hands up like he was surrenderin'. "Carmen, please, I didn't mean for this to happen. It was a mistake, I swear. I was drunk, I wasn't thinkin'."

"A mistake?" Carmen hissed, her voice drippin' with venom. "You think sleepin' with another woman is a mistake? You think betrayin' me like this is a fuckin' mistake?"

Travis stepped forward, his face pleadin', his eyes filled with tears. "Baby, please, I'm sorry. I fucked up, I know I did. But I love you, Carmen. I love you more than anything. Don't leave me, please. Don't leave me."

But Carmen was done. She was done with the lies, done with the bullshit, done with Travis. She couldn't believe she'd let herself get this far, let herself believe in his empty promises. She turned, runnin' out of the apartment, her vision blurred by tears, her heart achin' with every step.

She didn't know where she was goin', didn't care. She just needed to get away, needed to escape the pain, the betrayal, the humiliation. She could hear Travis callin' after her, his voice desperate, but she didn't look back. She couldn't. Not now. Not ever.

Carmen kept runnin' until her legs gave out, collapsin' on a bench in a small park, her body wracked with sobs. She couldn't stop cryin', couldn't stop the tears from fallin'. She felt like she was drownin', suffocatin' under the weight of her own heartbreak. She'd given everything to Travis, believed in him, loved him with all her heart, and this was how he repaid her.

She sat there for hours, lettin' the tears flow, lettin' the pain consume her. She thought about all the times she'd defended him, all the times she'd told herself he was different, that he could change. She thought about the dreams they'd shared, the future they'd planned, and how it had all been a lie.

When she finally pulled herself together, she knew what she had to do. She pulled out her phone, scrollin' through her contacts until she found Travis's number. With a deep breath, she pressed the block button, watchin' as his name disappeared from her screen. It was over. She was done.

Over the next few days, Carmen cut herself off from the world. She didn't go to work, didn't go to class, didn't talk to anyone. She stayed in her apartment, curtains drawn, hidin' from the outside world. She couldn't face anyone, couldn't deal with the questions, the pity, the judgment. She felt ashamed, embarrassed, like a fool for believin' in him.

She spent hours sittin' on her couch, starin' at the wall, replayin' the events of that night over and over in her head. She thought about all the red flags she'd ignored, all the times she'd chosen to look the other way. She thought about how far she'd strayed from her original path, from the person she used to be.

She remembered the girl she was before Travis came into her life—the girl with dreams, with ambitions, with a plan for her future. That girl was gone now, lost in the chaos and drama of Travis's world. Carmen didn't recognize herself anymore. She didn't know who she was without him, without the love she'd poured into their relationship.

But as the days went by, a new feelin' started to creep in, a feelin' she hadn't felt in a long time—anger. She was angry at Travis for what he'd done, for how he'd treated her, but more than that, she was angry at herself for lettin' it happen. She was angry for lettin' him control her, for lettin' him make her feel like she wasn't enough.

Carmen knew she couldn't keep livin' like this, couldn't keep drownin' in her own misery. She had to pick herself up, had to move on, had to find a way to heal. She had to find a way back to the girl she used to be, the girl who knew her worth, who didn't take shit from no one.

One night, as she sat on her bed, starin' out the window at the city lights, she made a decision. She was done cryin', done feelin' sorry for herself. She was done lettin' Travis dictate her life. She was gonna take back control, gonna find her own way, gonna be her own damn hero.

Carmen took a deep breath, feelin' a new sense of determination wash over her. She didn't know what the future held, didn't know how she was gonna move on, but she knew one thing for sure: she wasn't gonna let Travis or anyone else break her. She was stronger than that. She was better than that.

And as she closed her eyes, lettin' the tears fall one last time, she knew she was ready to start again. Ready to rebuild, ready to find herself, ready to face whatever came next. Because she was Carmen, and she wasn't gonna let no man define her.

Not now. Not ever.

Chapter 11: Family Intervention

Carmen hadn't seen her family in weeks, avoiding their calls and texts, not wanting to face them. She knew they were worried, knew they had questions she didn't have answers to. But after everything with Travis, she couldn't bring herself to be around anyone, especially not the people who knew her best. She was embarrassed, ashamed of how far she'd fallen.

One day, there was a knock at her door, loud and insistent. Carmen groaned, rolling over on the couch, hoping whoever it was would just go away. She wasn't in the mood for company, didn't want to see anyone. But the knocking continued, louder this time, and she knew she couldn't ignore it forever.

Reluctantly, she got up, dragging her feet across the floor as she went to the door. When she opened it, she found herself face-to-face with her mother, her older sister Lisa, and her aunt Debra. They all looked at her with a mix of concern and frustration, their eyes searching her face, trying to read her.

"Mama, what you doin' here?" Carmen asked, her voice barely above a whisper. "I ain't feelin' good. I just wanna be alone."

Her mother pushed past her, stepping into the small apartment, her face set in a firm line. "Baby, we been callin' you for days. You can't just shut us out like this. We family. We here to help you, not to judge you."

Lisa followed her mother inside, crossing her arms over her chest, her expression stern. "Carmen, you look like shit. What the hell is goin' on with you? You been actin' all weird, missin' work, ditchin' school. This ain't you."

Carmen closed the door, leaning against it, feeling the weight of their concern pressing down on her. "I'm fine, okay? I just... I just need some time."

But they weren't buying it. Aunt Debra, always the blunt one, stepped forward, her hands on her hips. "Girl, don't give us that bullshit. We know somethin' happened with Travis. We heard about it. Heard you caught him with some other chick. You think we don't know what's goin' on?"

Carmen flinched at the mention of Travis, her eyes welling up with tears. She didn't want to talk about it, didn't want to relive the pain. But she could see the worry in their eyes, the love, and it broke her. She couldn't keep it all bottled up anymore. She couldn't keep pretending everything was okay.

She sank to the floor, her shoulders shaking as the tears started to flow. "I don't know what to do, Mama," she sobbed, her voice cracking. "I thought he loved me. I thought... I thought we had somethin' real. But he lied to me. He played me like a damn fool."

Her mother knelt beside her, wrapping her arms around her, holding her tight. "Oh, baby, I'm so sorry," she murmured, her voice filled with pain. "I knew he was trouble. I knew he was gonna hurt you, but I didn't know how bad. I didn't know..."

Lisa joined them on the floor, her hand rubbing Carmen's back, trying to comfort her. "We just want you to be happy, Carmen. We want you to see your worth, to know you deserve better than some no-good street thug. You got so much potential, so much to offer. Don't let him take that away from you."

Aunt Debra nodded, her expression softening. "Lisa's right. You too smart, too good for that low life. You need to get back on track, focus on your studies, your future. Don't let him drag you down."

Carmen wiped her eyes, sniffling, feeling the weight of their words. She knew they were right. She knew she needed to get back on track, to find herself again. But it was hard. So damn hard. She felt like she was drowning, like she couldn't breathe, couldn't see a way out.

"I just feel so lost," she admitted, her voice barely a whisper. "I don't know who I am anymore. I don't know how to fix this."

Her mother squeezed her tighter, her voice soft but firm. "You don't have to do it alone, Carmen. We here for you. We love you. We just want to see you happy, to see you livin' the life you deserve. You can't do that if you still stuck on Travis."

Carmen nodded, taking a shaky breath. She knew her family was right. She needed to let go, needed to move on. But she didn't know how. She didn't know where to start.

Lisa grabbed her hands, her eyes serious. "First thing you gotta do is cut him off, for good. No more calls, no more texts, nothin'. Block his ass on everything. You need to focus on you, on gettin' your life back together. You can't do that if he's still in the picture."

Carmen hesitated, her heart aching at the thought of never talking to Travis again. But she knew it was the only way. She couldn't keep holding on to a man who didn't respect her, who didn't see her worth.

"Okay," she said finally, her voice trembling. "I'll do it. I'll block him. I just... I need y'all to help me. I can't do this by myself."

Her mother nodded, brushing a strand of hair away from Carmen's face. "Of course, baby. We got you. We always got you. You just gotta let us in, let us help you."

Aunt Debra stood up, her hands on her hips. "And you gotta get back to school, start focusin' on your future again. Ain't no man worth throwin' your life away for. You got too much goin' for you to let some fool ruin it."

Carmen nodded again, feeling a flicker of determination deep in her chest. She needed to take control, needed to find her way back. She couldn't keep living in the past, couldn't keep holding on to the pain. She had to move forward, had to find a way to heal.

Her family stayed with her the rest of the day, helping her clean up the apartment, making her eat something, talking to her about anything and everything to keep her mind off Travis. It felt good to have them there, to feel their support, their love. She hadn't realized how much she needed it, how much she'd missed it.

As the sun began to set, casting a warm glow through the window, Carmen sat on the couch, her phone in her hand, staring at Travis's number in the block box. She took a deep breath, her finger hovering over her phone. This was it. The final goodbye. She knew it was what she needed to do, knew it was the only way to truly move on.

With a trembling hand, she pressed the delete button, watching as his name disappeared from her screen. It felt like a weight had been lifted off her shoulders, like she could finally breathe again. She wasn't sure what the future held, wasn't sure how long it would take to heal, but she knew she was ready to start. She was ready to take control of her life again.

Her mother sat down beside her, wrapping an arm around her shoulders. "I'm proud of you, Carmen. I know this ain't easy, but you gonna get through this. We all here for you, every step of the way."

Lisa nodded, sitting on her other side, squeezing her hand. "Yeah, girl. We ain't lettin' you go down like that. You stronger than you think. And we gon' make sure you remember that."

Aunt Debra chimed in from across the room, her voice firm but kind. "And don't you forget, you a Harris. We don't let nobody walk all over us. You gon' come out of this stronger than ever, I know it."

Carmen smiled, feeling a warmth spread through her chest. She wasn't alone. She had her family, had people who loved her, who wanted to see her succeed. She wasn't sure where to go from here, wasn't sure how to pick up the pieces, but she knew she could do it. With them by her side, she could do anything.

As the night wore on, they stayed up late, talking, laughing, reminiscing about old times. For the first time in a long time, Carmen felt a glimmer of hope, felt like maybe, just maybe, she could find her way back. She knew it wouldn't be easy, knew she had a long road ahead, but she was ready to face it. She was ready to fight for herself, for her future.

And as she lay in bed that night, listening to the soft hum of the city outside her window, she made a promise to herself. She was done with Travis, done with the lies, the betrayal, the pain. She was gonna focus on herself, on her dreams, on her future. She was gonna be the woman she knew she could be, the woman she wanted to be.

Because she was Carmen Harris, and she was stronger than she ever knew. She was ready to take on the world, one step at a time. And with her family by her side, she knew she could do it. She knew she would come out on top, no matter what.

As she closed her eyes, a small smile on her lips, she felt a sense of peace wash over her, a feeling she hadn't felt in a

long time. She was ready. Ready to start again, ready to find herself, ready to be the best damn version of herself she could be. And this time, nothing was gonna stand in her way. Nothing.

Chapter 12: The Illusion of Change

Carmen had finally started to feel like she was getting her life back on track. Her family had rallied around her, giving her the strength she needed to move on from Travis. She blocked & deleted his number, cut him off completely, and threw herself back into her studies and work. But it wasn't long before Travis found a way to worm his way back into her life.

One evening, Carmen was walking home from the corner store, the sun dipping below the horizon, casting long shadows over the cracked pavement. Her phone buzzed in her pocket. She pulled it out, her heart skipping a beat when she saw Unknown flashing on the screen. She'd blocked his number, but he must have found another way to reach her.

Against her better judgment, she answered, her voice cold. "What do you want, Travis?"

"Carmen, please, just hear me out," he pleaded, his voice breaking. "I know I fucked up. I know I hurt you. But I swear, I'm ready to change. I'm ready to leave the streets behind, start fresh, be the man you need me to be."

Carmen's heart tightened in her chest. She wanted to hang up, wanted to tell him to go to hell, but she couldn't. His voice, that damn voice, always had a way of pulling her back in. "I don't know, Travis. I don't know if I can trust you again."

"I'm begging you, baby," Travis continued, desperation creeping into his tone. "I'm done with all that shit. I swear on everything, I'm done. Just give me one more chance. Let me prove to you that I can be different can I come by and talk to you later?"

Carmen stood there, her mind racing, her emotions a tangled mess. She knew she should say no, should walk away and never look back. But she also knew how much she still loved him, how much she wanted to believe he could change.

"Alright," she said softly, her resolve crumbling. "But this is it, Travis. If you fuck up again I will never give you the opportunity again. I mean it this time."

Travis's voice lit up with relief. "Thank you, Carmen. You won't regret this. I promise, I'm gonna make it right. I'm gonna make us right."

Despite her better judgment, Carmen found herself meeting up with Travis later that night. He showed up at her place with a bouquet of roses, a shy smile on his face. He looked different, more vulnerable, like he was genuinely trying to make amends.

They talked for hours, sitting on her couch, the city lights flickering outside the window. Travis told her about how he was ready to turn his life around, how he wanted to leave the streets behind and start over. He talked about getting a real job, about going back to school, about being a better man. Carmen listened, her heart aching with a mix of hope and doubt. She wanted to believe him, wanted to think that maybe, just maybe, he was telling the truth this time.

Over the next few weeks, things started to change. Travis kept his word, cutting ties with his old crew, spending more time with Carmen, and talking about their future. They went on long walks through the park, had quiet dinners at her apartment, and spent lazy Sundays watching movies on the couch.

For the first time in a long time, Carmen felt a glimmer of happiness, a sense of peace she hadn't felt from him in months. She started to think that maybe things could be different, that maybe Travis really was ready to change.

One night, as they were lying in bed, Travis turned to her, his eyes soft in the dim light. "I'm serious about this, Carmen," he said quietly, his voice filled with sincerity. "I want to be with you. I want to build a life with you, away from all the bullshit. I'm done with the streets, for real this time."

Carmen looked into his eyes, searching for any hint of deception, any sign that he was lying. But all she saw was honesty, a deep longing to be better, to be the man she needed him to be. "I believe you, Travis," she whispered, her voice thick with emotion. "I want that too. I want a future with you, without all the drama, without all the pain."

Travis smiled, pulling her close, his lips brushing against her forehead. "Then that's what we're gonna have, baby. I promise you. I'm gonna make it happen."

For a while, it seemed like things were actually different. Travis was around more, spending time with Carmen, helping her with her studies, even talking about getting a job at a local mechanic shop. Carmen's friends and family started to notice the change in her, the way her smile seemed more genuine, the lightness in her step. They were cautious, but they could see that she was happy, and they wanted to believe that maybe, just maybe, Travis had finally turned a corner.

But there was always a lingering unease, a nagging doubt that Carmen couldn't shake. She knew Travis's past, knew the kind of life he'd lived, and she couldn't help but wonder if he could really leave it all behind. She wanted to believe in him, wanted to believe that their love was strong enough to overcome anything, but the shadows of their past loomed large, casting a dark cloud over their newfound happiness.

One evening, as they were walking on an evening stroll, Travis's phone rang. He glanced at the screen, his face tightening for a split second before he put it away, ignoring the call. Carmen noticed, a knot forming in her stomach.

"Who was that?" she asked, trying to keep her voice casual.

"Just a friend," Travis replied quickly, a little too quickly. "Nothin' important."

Carmen nodded, but the unease was there, simmering beneath the surface. She didn't want to push him, didn't want to ruin the good thing they had going, but she couldn't shake the feeling that something was off.

Over the next few days, Carmen started to notice little things—Travis's sudden disappearances, the way he'd get quiet whenever his phone rang, those hushed conversations he'd have when he thought she wasn't around. She tried to ignore it, tried to focus on the good, but the doubts were creeping back in, wrapping around her heart like a vice.

One afternoon, Carmen decided to confront him, to ask him straight up what was going on. She found him sitting on the couch, flipping through channels, looking relaxed, like he didn't have a care in the world.

"Travis, we need to talk," she said, her voice firm, her hands trembling at her sides.

Travis looked up, his brow furrowing. "What's wrong, baby? You look upset."

Carmen took a deep breath, trying to steady herself. "I just... I need to know if you're serious about this. About us. About changing. I can't do this again, Travis. I can't go through all that pain again."

Travis sighed, leaning back against the couch, rubbing a hand over his face. "Carmen, I told you, I'm done with that life. I'm here with you, ain't I? I'm trying, baby. I'm really trying."

"I know you say that," Carmen replied, her voice wavering. "But I need to see it. I need to know you're not just telling me what I want to hear."

Travis got up, walking over to her, taking her hands in his. "I get it, Carmen. I do. And I'm gonna prove it to you. I'm gonna show you that I'm serious. Just give me a little more time, okay?"

Carmen nodded, her heart aching with a mix of hope and fear. She wanted to believe him, wanted to think that maybe, just maybe, this time would be different. But the doubts were still there, lingering in the shadows, waiting to pounce.

As the weeks went by, Carmen tried to push the doubts away, focusing on the good moments, the laughter, the love they shared. But no matter how hard she tried, the darkness was always there, lurking just beneath the surface, threatening to pull them under.

One night, as they were lying in bed, Travis's phone buzzed on the nightstand. He glanced at it, his face tightening, his hand reaching out to silence it. Carmen watched him, her heart sinking. She knew that look, knew that expression all too well.

"Travis, who is it?" she asked softly, her voice tinged with fear.

"Nobody," Travis muttered, turning away from her. "Just go back to sleep, Carmen. It's nothing."

But Carmen knew it wasn't nothing. She knew that the shadows were creeping back in, that the darkness was closing in around them. And as she lay there, staring up at the ceiling, she couldn't help but wonder if she'd ever really be free from it, if they'd ever truly escape the life that had brought them together, but also threatened to tear them apart.

Chapter 13: The Deeper Entanglement

Carmen thought she'd seen the worst of Travis's world, but she was wrong. For a while, things seemed good. Too good. Travis was doing everything right—staying close, keeping his promises, talking about their future like he meant it. But the streets had a way of pulling you back in, of holding onto you like quicksand, and it wasn't long before Travis started slipping.

It began with the late-night calls, the whispers Carmen pretended not to hear. She didn't ask questions, didn't want to know. She'd convinced herself that she could ignore it, that she could keep pretending everything was fine. But the truth was always there, lurking in the shadows, waiting to come crashing down.

One evening, Travis came home looking more tense than usual. His jaw was tight, his eyes darting around the room like he was expecting something bad to happen. Carmen noticed, but she kept her mouth shut, trying to keep the peace. But deep down, she knew. She knew something was wrong.

"What's goin' on, Travis?" she finally asked, her voice soft, hesitant. "You look like you got the weight of the world on your shoulders."

Travis glanced at her, his eyes dark and unreadable. "Nothin' you need to worry about, Carmen," he muttered, running a hand through his hair. "Just some old shit I gotta handle."

Carmen frowned, her heart sinking. "You told me you was done with all that. You told me you was out."

"I am out!" Travis snapped, his voice sharp. "But sometimes the streets don't let you go that easy. I'm handling it, a'ight? Just trust me."

But Carmen could see it in his face, could feel the tension radiating off him. She wanted to believe him, wanted to think he was telling the truth, but the doubt was there, gnawing at her, refusing to be ignored.

A few days later, Carmen found herself dragged into Travis's mess in the worst way. They were driving through the city, Travis's hand resting on the steering wheel, his eyes flicking to the rearview mirror every few seconds. Carmen could feel the anxiety rolling off him in waves, her own nerves starting to fray.

"Travis, where are we goin'?" she asked, her voice shaking. "Why are you actin' so weird?"

Travis didn't answer right away. He just kept driving, his jaw clenched, his grip on the wheel tightening. Finally, he pulled into an alley, killing the engine. He turned to Carmen, his face serious.

"Listen, Carmen, I need you to stay in the car, a'ight? Don't get out. Don't ask questions. Just stay put."

Carmen's heart pounded in her chest, fear clawing at her throat. "Travis, what the hell is goin' on? You're scarin' me."

Travis leaned over, his hand cupping her cheek, his eyes softening for a moment. "I'm sorry, baby. I didn't want to bring you into this. But I gotta take care of some shit, and I need you to trust me. Can you do that?"

Carmen nodded, her eyes wide, her breath catching in her throat. She wanted to trust him, wanted to believe that he had everything under control. But deep down, she knew. She knew this was a bad idea.

Travis got out of the car, leaving Carmen alone in the darkness. She watched as he disappeared down the alley, her mind racing, her heart pounding in her ears. She wanted to call out to him, to beg him to come back, but she couldn't find her voice. She was frozen, paralyzed by fear.

Minutes passed, each one feeling like an eternity. Carmen's hands were shaking, her eyes darting around, searching for any sign of Travis. Then she heard it—the sound of raised voices, a scuffle, a gunshot echoing through the night. Her blood ran cold, panic clawing at her chest.

Without thinking, she jumped out of the car, running toward the sound, her heart in her throat. She rounded the corner, her breath hitching as she saw Travis standing over a man, a gun in his hand, his face twisted in anger.

"Travis, no!" she screamed, rushing forward, her hands reaching out to grab him. "What are you doin'? Stop!"

Travis looked up, his eyes wild, his chest heaving. "Carmen, get the fuck in the car! Now!"

But Carmen couldn't move. She was rooted to the spot, her mind reeling, her body trembling. She didn't know what to do, didn't know how to fix this. All she knew was that she was in way over her head, caught in a nightmare she couldn't escape.

"Please, Travis," she whispered, tears streaming down her face. "Just stop. We can leave, we can go somewhere, anywhere. Just leave all this behind."

Travis shook his head, his expression hardening. "It ain't that simple, Carmen. You don't understand."

Before she could say anything else, a car screeched into the alley, headlights blinding her. A group of men jumped out, guns drawn, shouting at Travis to drop his weapon. Carmen screamed, throwing herself in front of him, her arms outstretched.

"No, please! Don't shoot! He didn't mean it!"

But it was too late. Shots rang out, bullets tearing through the night, shattering the fragile peace that had hung between them. Carmen felt something hot and sharp slam into her side, pain exploding through her body. She stumbled, her vision blurring, her knees buckling beneath her.

Travis caught her as she fell, his arms wrapping around her, his voice frantic, desperate. "Carmen! No, no, no! Stay with me, baby! Stay with me!"

Carmen's world was spinning, her head swimming, her body going numb. She could hear Travis's voice, but it sounded far away, like he was underwater. She wanted to tell him she was okay, that she'd be fine, but she couldn't speak. She couldn't move. Everything was slipping away.

When she woke up, she was in a hospital bed, her side bandaged, an IV in her arm. Her head was pounding, her mouth dry, her throat raw.

She blinked, trying to focus, trying to remember what had happened. Then it all came rushing back—the alley, the gunshots, Travis's face twisted with fear.

Her mother was sitting by her side, holding her hand, tears streaming down her cheeks. "Oh, thank God, you're awake," she whispered, squeezing Carmen's hand. "We were so scared, baby. We thought we'd lost you."

Carmen's eyes filled with tears, her heart breaking all over again. "Mama, I'm so sorry," she choked out, her voice barely a whisper. "I didn't mean for this to happen. I didn't know..."

Her mother shook her head, her face full of pain. "Shh, it's okay, Carmen. It's okay. You're safe now. That's all that matters."

But Carmen knew it wasn't okay. Nothing was okay. She'd almost died because of Travis, because of the choices she'd made, because she couldn't let go. She'd put herself in danger, put her family through hell, all for a man who couldn't see past his own demons.

As the days went by, Carmen's friends started to distance themselves, fed up with her constant drama, her refusal to listen to reason. They didn't understand why she kept going back to Travis, why she couldn't just walk away. And honestly, Carmen didn't know either. She felt more isolated than ever, alone with her thoughts, her regrets, her broken heart.

And then there were the women. They started coming out of the woodwork, each one claiming they were involved with Travis, that he'd promised them the same things he'd promised Carmen. It was like a punch to the gut, a reminder of just how deep his lies went, how far he was willing to go to get what he wanted.

Carmen tried to shut it all out, tried to focus on healing, on moving on. But it was hard. Harder than she ever thought it would be. She felt like she was drowning, suffocating under the weight of her own mistakes, her own choices. She didn't know how to climb out of the hole she'd dug herself into, didn't know if she even wanted to.

But as she lay in that hospital bed, staring up at the ceiling, listening to the beep of the heart monitor, she knew one thing for sure: she couldn't keep living like this. She couldn't keep letting Travis drag her down, keep letting his world consume her. She had to find a way out, had to find a way to save herself, before it was too late.

And as she closed her eyes, a tear slipping down her cheek, she made a promise to herself: she was done with Travis, done with his lies, his games, his bullshit. She was going to find a way to get out, to get clean, to find herself again. No matter what it took. No matter how hard it was.

Because she was Carmen, and she was stronger than this. She had to be. She had to find a way to survive. She was on her way home but she had almost lost her life and that was not okay.

Chapter 14: The Big Bust

It was early morning, the sun barely peeking through the blinds, casting long shadows across the room. Carman was just home from the hospital and was still groggy, her mind foggy from sleep when she heard the commotion outside. Voices shouting, heavy footsteps pounding up the stairs, the sound of doors being slammed open.

Her heart leapt into her throat as she scrambled out of bed, rushing to the window. She peeked through the blinds, her breath catching in her throat at the sight below. Police cars filled the street, their lights flashing red and blue, officers in tactical gear swarming the building. She could hear them shouting, barking orders, their guns drawn, ready for anything.

"Fuck," she whispered, her hands trembling as she backed away from the window. "What the hell is going on?"

She grabbed her phone, frantically dialing Travis's number, but it went straight to voicemail. Panic clawed at her chest, her mind racing. She didn't know what to do, didn't know how to get out. She was trapped, caught in the middle of something she didn't understand, something she never wanted to be a part of.

Just as she was about to try and make a run for it, the door burst open, a group of officers flooding into the room, their guns raised. "Police! Get down on the ground!" one of them shouted, his voice booming.

Carmen froze, her hands going up in the air, her eyes wide with fear. "I—I didn't do anything!" she cried, her voice trembling. "I don't know what's going on!"

"Down on the ground, now!" the officer barked, stepping forward, his gun still trained on her.

Carmen dropped to her knees, her heart hammering in her chest, her breath coming in short, panicked gasps. She could feel tears streaming down her face, her whole body shaking. She'd never been this scared in her life, never felt so helpless, so lost.

They grabbed her, pulling her arms behind her back, slapping handcuffs on her wrists. She winced, the fresh gunshot wounds and then there was metal biting into her skin, her mind spinning. They dragged her out of the apartment, down the stairs, and into the street, where more officers were waiting.

She looked around, trying to make sense of the chaos, but it was too much. Everything was a blur—the flashing lights, the shouting, the sea of uniforms. She caught a glimpse of Travis being led out of the building, his hands cuffed behind his back, his face grim, his eyes hard. He didn't look at her, didn't say a word, just kept his head down, moving forward.

"Travis!" Carmen screamed, her voice breaking, desperate. "Travis, what's happening? What's going on?"

But he didn't respond. He didn't even turn around. Carmen felt a sense of betrayal, her heart breaking all over again. She was alone, completely alone, and she didn't know what to do.

They shoved her into the back of a police car, slamming the door shut behind her. She sat there, staring out the window, her mind numb, her body shaking. She couldn't believe this was happening. She couldn't believe she was caught up in this mess, that she was in the middle of a police raid, that her life had spiraled so far out of control.

The ride to the station was a blur. Carmen sat there in stunned silence, her thoughts racing, her heart heavy with dread. She had no idea what was going to happen, no idea what she was going to do. All she knew was that she was in deep, way deeper than she'd ever imagined.

When they got to the station, they pulled her out of the car, leading her inside, down a long hallway, and into a small, cold room with a metal table and two chairs. They sat her down, un-cuffing her hands, telling her to wait. She sat there, her hands shaking, her eyes wide, her breath coming in shallow gasps.

Minutes felt like hours as she waited, alone in that room, her mind spinning. She thought about Travis, about the choices she'd made, about how she'd gotten here. She thought about her family, her friends, everyone she'd pushed away, everyone she'd hurt. She thought about all the times she'd ignored the warning signs, all the times she'd chosen to look the other way.

She was so lost in her thoughts that she didn't hear the door open. She jumped, her head snapping up as a detective walked in, his face stern, his eyes cold. He sat down across from her, folding his hands on the table, staring at her for a long moment before speaking.

"Miss Harris, I'm Detective Johnson," he said, his voice calm but firm. "Do you know why you're here?"

Carmen shook her head, her voice barely a whisper. "No, I don't... I don't know what's going on. I don't know why I'm here."

The detective nodded, his expression unreadable. "We have reason to believe that you've been involved in some criminal activities, specifically related to Travis Brown and his operation. We need to ask you some questions about what you know, about what you've seen."

Carmen's heart sank, her stomach twisting into knots. "I—I don't know anything," she stammered, her voice shaking. "I swear, I didn't know what he was doing. I didn't know..."

"Miss Harris," Detective Johnson interrupted, his voice sharp. "We're not here to play games. This is serious. We have evidence linking you to Travis's activities. We need you to be honest with us, or things could get a lot worse for you."

Carmen's mind reeled, her heart pounding in her chest. She felt like she was suffocating, like the walls were closing in around her. She didn't know what to say, didn't know how to make them believe her. She was scared, more scared than she'd ever been in her life.

"Please," she whispered, tears streaming down her face. "I didn't do anything. I didn't know what he was doing. I just... I just wanted to help him. I thought I could help him..."

The detective watched her, his eyes narrowing. "Help him? Help him with what, Miss Harris?"

Carmen hesitated, her mind racing. She didn't know what to say, didn't know how much to tell him. She didn't want to make things worse, didn't want to dig herself into a deeper hole.

"I thought I could help him get out," she finally said, her voice barely a whisper. "I thought I could help him leave the streets, start fresh. I didn't know how deep he was in. I didn't know..."

Detective Johnson leaned back in his chair, his eyes never leaving her. "And did you ever think about what that meant for you, Miss Harris? Did you ever think about the consequences of getting involved with someone like Travis Brown?"

Carmen shook her head, tears blurring her vision. "I didn't think... I didn't think it would come to this. I didn't think I'd be here, talking to you. I just... I just wanted to help him."

The detective sighed, running a hand through his hair. "Miss Harris, I believe you. I believe you didn't know what you were getting into. But that doesn't change the fact that you're involved, whether you like it or not. You're in deep, and you need to understand that."

Carmen nodded, her heart heavy with regret. She knew he was right. She knew she'd made a mistake, that she'd let herself get pulled into a world she didn't understand, a world that was dangerous and dark.

After what felt like hours, they finally let her go, telling her she was free to leave, but that they might need to speak with her again. She stumbled out of the station, her mind numb, her body aching. She felt like she was walking in a daze, like she was trapped in a nightmare she couldn't wake up from.

When she got home, she collapsed on her bed, tears streaming down her face, her heart breaking all over again. She felt more lost than ever, more confused, more scared. She didn't know what to do, didn't know how to move forward.

She thought about Travis, about the life he led, about the choices he'd made. She thought about how deeply she'd gotten entangled in his world, how much she'd sacrificed for him, how much she'd lost. She thought about all the times she'd told herself she could change him, that she could be his anchor, his savior. But now, she knew the truth. She knew that he was beyond saving, and that she was too, if she didn't find a way out.

As the sun set outside her window, casting long shadows across the room, Carmen made a decision. She had to be done with Travis, done with his lies, his games, his world. She was going to find a way to get out, to start fresh, to rebuild her life. She didn't know how, didn't know where to start, but she knew she had to try.

And as she lay there, staring up at the ceiling, her mind racing, her heart heavy, she made a promise to herself: she was going to survive this. She was going to find a way to get through this, to come out stronger on the other side. Because she wasn't going to let anyone, not even Travis, destroy her.

Chapter 15: The Breaking News

The whole neighborhood was buzzin' with gossip. Word spread fast about the raid, about Travis gettin' snatched up by the cops, about Carmen bein' right there in the thick of it. It seemed like everybody had somethin' to say, and none of it was good. Carmen felt like she was livin' under a microscope, every move she made bein' scrutinized, judged.

She couldn't even step out her front door without hearin' the whispers, feelin' the side-eye glances. "Ain't that Carmen? The girl who got caught up with Travis? Heard she was runnin' with him, right up till they busted his ass." The words cut like knives, leavin' her raw and bleedin'. She knew she'd fucked up, knew she'd let herself get dragged into a world she had no business bein' in, but hearin' it from everybody else, it was like pourin' salt in an open wound.

She tried to keep her head down, to ignore the stares and the talk, but it wasn't easy. Everywhere she went, it felt like people were watchin' her, judgin' her, like she was somethin' dirty they didn't wanna get too close to. It seemed everybody, the ones who'd stuck by her through everything, started to pull away. They didn't say it outright, but she could see it in their eyes, hear it in their voices. They were tired, fed up with the drama, with the constant chaos that came with bein' around her.

Carmen found herself more alone than ever, trapped in her own thoughts, her own regrets. She thought about Travis, about how everything had spiraled out of control, about how she'd ended up here, in this mess, with no way out. She missed him, missed the good times they'd had, but she also felt a strange sense of relief. With him behind bars, she didn't have to worry about the late-night calls, the shady shit, the danger lurkin' around every corner. For the first time in a long time, she could breathe.

But the relief was short-lived. The shame, the guilt, the embarrassment—they were always there, lurkin' just beneath the surface, ready to swallow her whole. She couldn't escape it, couldn't outrun it. Everywhere she turned, there was a reminder of what she'd lost, of what she'd done.

One afternoon, Carmen was at the corner store, tryin' to pick up a few things, keepin' her head down, hopin' nobody would notice her. But she wasn't that lucky. She heard the whispers, the snickers, the not-so-quiet comments as she moved through the aisles.

"Look, there she go. Can you believe she's still out here, actin' like she ain't got no shame?"

"I heard she was all up in Travis's business, helpin' him with his deals. She lucky she ain't locked up too."

Carmen clenched her fists, her heart poundin' in her chest. She wanted to scream, wanted to shout at them, tell them they didn't know shit, that they didn't know what she'd been through, what she'd sacrificed. But she kept her mouth shut, her head down, grabbin' her things and leavin' as fast as she could.

Back at her apartment, Carmen sat on the couch, her head in her hands, her mind racin'. She felt like she was at a crossroads, like she had to make a choice. She could try to move on, to leave Travis and his world behind, or she could wait, hope that things would change once he got out, hope that he'd finally be ready to start fresh, to be the man she'd always wanted him to be.

But deep down, she knew the truth. Travis wasn't gonna change. He was who he was, and no matter how much she wanted to believe he could be different, she couldn't ignore the reality. He was in deep, caught up in a life that was dangerous, destructive, a life that had almost cost her everything.

As she sat there, starin' out the window, watchin' the city lights flicker in the distance, Carmen felt a tear roll down her cheek. She didn't know what to do, didn't know how to move forward. She felt lost, adrift, like she was floatin' in the middle of a storm with no way to reach the shore.

Her phone buzzed on the table, breakin' through her thoughts. She picked it up, her heart skippin' a beat when she saw the message from Travis. She hadn't heard from him since the raid, hadn't known if he'd even try to reach out. But there it was, his name flashin' on the screen. There was his text.

I'm sorry, Carmen. I fucked up. Can we talk? I need to explain.

Carmen stared at the screen, her hands shakin', her heart achin'. She wanted to believe him, wanted to think that maybe this time would be different, that maybe he'd finally seen the light. But she knew better. She knew it was just another empty promise, another lie he was tellin' himself as much as he was tellin' her.

She put the phone down, takin' a deep breath, tryin' to steady herself. She knew she had to make a decision, knew she couldn't keep goin' back and forth, lettin' him pull her into his world over and over again. She had to choose—him or her, the past or the future.

The next day, Carmen decided to take a walk, to clear her head, to think about what she really wanted. She walked through the neighborhood, passin' by the places she and Travis used to hang out, the spots that held so many memories, both good and bad. She thought about all the times she'd defended him, all the times she'd told herself he could change, that he just needed time, needed her.

But as she walked, she realized somethin'. She couldn't keep waitin' for him to change, couldn't keep puttin' her life on hold, hopin' he'd finally be the man she needed him to be. She had to let go, had to move on, had to find a way to live for herself.

When she got back to her apartment, she sat down at the kitchen table, her mind made up. She had to walk away and stand on that!

Over the next few weeks, Carmen threw herself into her work, her studies, tryin' to focus on the things that mattered, the things that would help her move forward. She started spendin' more time with her family, reconnectin' with old friends, tryin' to rebuild the bridges she'd burned.

It wasn't easy. The gossip, the stares, the whispers—they were still there, still followin' her wherever she went. But she tried to ignore them, tried to keep her head up, to remind herself that she was stronger than all of it, stronger than the mistakes she'd made, stronger than the past.

One afternoon, as she was walkin' home from the store, she saw Mariah, her best friend from before everything went to shit. They hadn't spoken in months, hadn't seen each other since Carmen had started messin' with Travis. But there she was, standin' on the corner, watchin' Carmen with a mix of sadness and relief.

"Hey, Mariah," Carmen said softly, her voice tinged with regret. "I'm sorry, for everything. I know I fucked up. I just... I miss you."

Mariah looked at her for a long moment, her eyes softening, her expression unreadable. "I miss you too, Carmen," she said finally, her voice barely above a whisper. "But you gotta get your shit together. You gotta do better. For you, not for him."

Carmen nodded, tears fillin' her eyes. "I know. I'm tryin'. I really am."

Mariah gave her a small smile, reachin' out to squeeze her hand. "I'm here, if you need me. Just don't fuck up again, okay?"

Carmen laughed through her tears, noddin' again. "I won't. I promise."

As they stood there, holdin' each other's gaze, Carmen felt a flicker of hope, a sense of peace she hadn't felt in a long time. She knew she had a long way to go, knew she still had a lot of healin' to do, but she also knew she wasn't alone. She had people who cared about her, people who wanted to see her succeed, and that was enough. That was more than enough.

And as she walked away, her heart lighter, her mind clearer, she knew she was ready to face whatever came next. She was ready to take control of her life, to find her own path, to be the woman she knew she could be. Because she was Carmen Harris, and she was stronger than she ever knew. She was ready to take on the world, one step at a time.

Chapter 16: The Revelations

Carmen had told herself she was done with Travis. She'd blocked his number again, cut him out, tried to move on with her life. She hadn't seen him in weeks, and despite everything, she couldn't shake the memories of the good times, the moments when he'd made her feel like she was the only one in the world.

She knew she shouldn't even talk to him and by doing so she knew she was only setting herself up for more pain. But when he showed up at her doorstep, lookin' broken and desperate, she couldn't turn him away. She let him in, let him wrap his arms around her, let him whisper apologies and promises that she knew were empty. She wanted to believe him, wanted to think that maybe this time, things would be different.

"Carmen, baby, I'm sorry," Travis murmured, his voice thick with emotion. "I know I fucked up, I know I hurt you, but I swear, I'm ready to make it right. I just need you to give me one more chance."

Carmen looked into his eyes, searchin' for somethin' real, somethin' true. She saw the pain, the regret, but she also saw the lies, the deceit, the darkness that had always been there. She wanted to push him away, wanted to tell him to leave, but she couldn't. She was too tired, too worn down, too broken.

"Why should I believe you, Travis?" she asked softly, her voice barely a whisper. "Why should I think this time is any different?"

Travis sighed, runnin' a hand through her hair, his eyes fillin' with tears. "Because I'm tellin' you the truth, Carmen. I'm layin' it all out there. No more lies, no more bullshit. I'm ready to come clean, to tell you everything."

Carmen's heart tightened in her chest, a knot forming in her stomach. "Everything? What do you mean, everything?"

Travis looked away, his jaw clenching, his hands balling into fists at his sides. "I mean about the other women. About all the shit I've been doin' behind your back. I ain't proud of it, but you deserve to know. You deserve to hear the truth."

Carmen felt like she'd been punched in the gut, her breath catchin' in her throat. She'd known, deep down, that Travis had been unfaithful, but hearin' him say it, hearin' him admit it, was like a knife to the heart. "How many, Travis?" she whispered, her voice shaking. "How many women?"

Travis hesitated, his eyes dartin' around the room, like he was lookin' for an escape. "I don't know," he said finally, his voice low. "A few. More than a few. I lost count. I was reckless, Carmen. I was stupid. I didn't think. I just... I just did what I wanted, without thinkin' about you, about us about the bigger picture."

Carmen's eyes filled with tears, her body trembling. "You lost count?" she repeated, her voice rising, her anger boiling over. "You lost fuckin' count, Travis? How could you do that to me? How could you lie to me, cheat on me, over and over again?"

Travis hung his head, his shoulders slumpin', his face filled with shame. "I don't know, Carmen. I don't know why I did it. I guess... I guess I thought I could get away with it. I thought I could have my cake and eat it too. I was wrong. I was so fuckin' wrong."

Carmen felt like her world was collapsing around her, like everything she'd believed in, everything she'd held onto, was crumbling to dust. She'd known Travis wasn't perfect, known he had a dark side, but she'd always thought he loved her, thought he'd never do somethin' like this. "Do you even know what you've done to me?" she cried, her voice breaking, tears streaming down her face. "Do you even care?"

Travis reached out, tryin' to touch her, but she slapped his hand away, her anger flaring. "Don't touch me! Don't fuckin' touch me!"

"I'm sorry, Carmen," Travis pleaded, his voice cracking, his eyes desperate. "I know I hurt you. I know I fucked up. But I love you. I love you more than anything. I need you. I need you to forgive me, to give me another chance."

Carmen shook her head, her heart shattering. "How can you say you love me, Travis? How can you say that when you've been sleepin' with other women, when you've been lyin' to me, makin' me look like a damn fool?"

Travis stepped back, his face pale, his eyes wide with panic. "I don't know, Carmen. I don't know what's wrong with me. I just... I just wanted to feel somethin', to feel alive. I didn't think about what it would do to you, to us."

Carmen felt like she couldn't breathe, like the walls were closin' in on her. She wanted to scream, to cry, to run away, but she couldn't move. She was trapped, caught in a web of lies and betrayal, and she didn't know how to get out. "You're a fuckin' coward, Travis," she spat, her voice dripping with venom. "You're a selfish, pathetic coward."

Travis flinched, his face contorting with pain. "I know," he whispered, his voice barely audible. "I know I am. But I want to be better, Carmen. I want to be the man you deserve. I just... I just don't know how."

Carmen turned away, her heart heavy, her mind numb. She didn't know what to do, didn't know how to move forward. She felt like she was drowning, like she was bein' pulled under by the weight of her own pain. "I can't do this, Travis," she said softly, her voice trembling. "I can't keep lettin' you hurt me, lettin' you drag me down. I deserve better than this. I deserve better than you."

Travis's face crumpled, his eyes fillin' with tears. "Please, Carmen, don't say that. Don't give up on me. I need you. I love you. Please, just give me one more chance."

But Carmen had heard enough. She'd given him too many chances, too many opportunities to change, to be the man she needed him to be. And he'd blown it, every single time. She couldn't keep holdin' on to a fantasy, couldn't keep lyin' to herself, tellin' herself that things would get better, that he would get better.

"No, Travis," she said firmly, her voice steady despite the tears streamin' down her face. "I'm done. I'm done with the lies, the cheating, the bullshit. I'm done with you."

She turned and walked away, her heart breakin' with every step, but she didn't look back. She couldn't. She knew if she did, she'd crumble, she'd fall right back into his arms, into his web of deceit and pain. She had to be strong, had to find a way to move on, to start over, to rebuild.

As she politely asked him to leave and she slammed the door behind him, Carmen felt a sense of finality, a sense of closure. She knew it wouldn't be easy, knew she had a long road ahead, but she was ready to face it, ready to take control of her life, to find herself again.

She was done with bein' a victim. She was ready to be a warrior, ready to fight for her own happiness, her own peace, her own life. And this time, she was gonna win. No matter what it took. No matter how hard it was.

Carmen felt a sense of freedom, a sense of hope. She didn't know what the future held, didn't know where she was headed, but she knew she was gonna be okay. She knew she was gonna make it, one way or another.

And for the first time in a long time, she felt like she was finally really ready to start again. Ready to find her own path, her own way, her own life. This shit was a wrap!

Chapter 17: Health Issues

Travis had been feelin' strange lately, and not just his usual running the streets strange. He was tired all the time, more than usual. He'd sleep for hours, barely drag himself outta bed, and even then, he'd just sit on the couch, lookin' like he was miles away. His boys had noticed it, the way he was sweatin' at night, the way his clothes started hangin' off him like they didn't fit right no more.

"Travis, you aight?" his friend Ty asked one morning, his voice filled with worry as he watched him struggle to lift his head from the pillow to make their daily runs.

"Yeah, yeah, I'm good," Travis muttered, wavin' him off. His face was pale, dark circles under his eyes makin' him look even worse. "Just stress, you know? All this shit goin' on. It's takin' a toll on me."

But Ty wasn't convinced. He knew Travis, knew when he was tryin' to brush shit off, pretend like everything was fine when it wasn't. And this wasn't fine. Not by a long shot.

"Travis, this ain't just stress," Ty said firmly, his eyes lockin' on his. "You been lookin' like hell for weeks. You ain't eatin', you ain't sleepin' right. You gotta see a doctor bruh."

Travis scoffed, rollin' his eyes. "Ain't nothin' wrong with me, Ty. I'm just tired. I need some rest, that's all."

But Ty wasn't havin' it. He could see he was scared, could see the fear in his eyes, even if he wouldn't admit it. He'd never seen him like this before, so vulnerable, so weak. And it scared him too.

"You goin' to the doctor, Travis," he insisted, his voice hard, leavin' no room for argument. "I don't care what you say. You gotta get checked out it could be Covid or anything too much shit floating around."

Travis looked at him, his jaw clenching, his eyes flickerin' with frustration. But he knew he was right. He knew he couldn't keep ignorin' it, couldn't keep pretendin' like everything was okay when it wasn't.

"Fine," he grumbled, finally givin' in. "I'll go. But I'm tellin' you, it's just stress. Ain't nothin' else."

Ty nodded, but deep down, he wasn't so sure. He had a bad feelin', a knot in his stomach that wouldn't go away. He hoped it was just stress, hoped it was somethin' that could be fixed with some rest, some time. But he couldn't shake the feelin' that it was somethin' more, somethin' worse cuz Travis looked badddd. Travis told Ty to call Carmen hoping that she would be concerned and would go with him to the doctor for moral support. And she decided to go with him with no hesitation because it was the right thing to do.

They went to the clinic a few days later, the air thick with tension. Travis sat in the waitin' room, his leg bouncin' up and down, his fingers drumming on the armrest. Carmen sat beside him, her hands clenched in her lap, her heart poundin' in her chest. She didn't know what to expect, didn't know what they were gonna hear, but she knew it wasn't gonna be good she hadn't seen him in a while and he looked awful.

When the doctor finally called them in, Travis stood up, takin' a deep breath, tryin' to gather himself. Carmen followed, her stomach twistin' into knots, her mind racin'. She could feel the fear radiatin' off him, feel it seepin' into her own skin, her own bones.

The doctor was a middle-aged man with glasses and a kind face, but his expression was serious as he looked at Travis, then at Carmen. "Mr. Brown," he began, his voice calm but firm. " We ran several tests trying to narrow down the issue with your illness and your symptoms. We got your test results back, and... I'm afraid it's not good news."

Carmen's heart stopped, her breath catchin' in her throat. She looked at Travis, her eyes wide, her mind screamin' for the doctor to just say it, to just tell them what was wrong.

"What... what is it?" Travis asked, his voice barely a whisper, his hands tremblin' at his sides.

The doctor sighed, glancin' down at the chart in his hands. "You're HIV positive, Mr. Brown. The symptoms you've been experiencing are consistent with early stages of the virus. I'm very sorry."

The words hit Carmen like a freight train, knockin' the wind outta her, leavin' her dizzy, her vision blurrin'. HIV. She couldn't believe it, couldn't wrap her mind around it. She looked at Travis, saw the shock, the fear, the pain on his face, and her heart broke all over again.

"N-no, that can't be right," Travis stammered, shakin' his head, his voice crackin'. "There's gotta be a mistake. I ain't got no HIV. I ain't sick."

"I'm afraid the tests don't lie," the doctor said gently, his eyes filled with sympathy. "But we can discuss treatment options, ways to manage the virus, to live a healthy life. It's not the end, Mr. Brown."

Carmen felt like she was underwater, like everything around her was muffled, distant. She heard the doctor talkin', heard him explainin' things, but she couldn't process it, couldn't make sense of it. All she could think about was Travis, about all the women he'd been with, about all the times he'd lied to her, cheated on her, betrayed her trust. And about her own health.

Travis looked at her, his face crumblin', his eyes filled with regret. "I didn't know, Carmen. I swear, I didn't know. I never meant for this to happen. I'm so fuckin' sorry."

But sorry wasn't enough. Sorry wasn't gonna change the fact that he'd put her at risk, that he'd been reckless, careless, that he'd destroyed everything they'd built, everything they'd been tryin' to build. She felt like her world was fallin' apart..

The doctor looked at Carmen, his expression serious. "Miss Harris, I'd recommend you get tested as well, given the circumstances. It's important to know where you stand, to take the necessary precautions."

Carmen nodded numbly, her mind still reelin', her heart poundin' in her chest. She followed the nurse out of the room, her legs feelin' like lead, her body numb. She didn't know how she made it through the test, didn't know how she kept it together, but somehow, she did. She sat there, waitin', the minutes stretchin' into hours, feelin' like a lifetime.

When the nurse finally came back, her expression was somber, her eyes filled with sympathy. "Miss Harris, I'm so sorry," she said softly, her voice gentle. "Your test came back positive as well. You're HIV positive."

Carmen felt like the floor had been ripped out from under her, like she was free-fallin' into an abyss with no end in sight. She couldn't breathe, couldn't think, couldn't move. She just sat there, numb, the words echoing in her mind, over and over again.

HIV positive.

She felt a hand on her shoulder, heard Travis's voice, distant, far away. "Carmen, I'm so sorry. I never wanted this for you. I never wanted any of this."

But she couldn't hear him, couldn't see him. She was lost, trapped in her own mind, in her own pain, in her own despair. She'd trusted him, loved him, believed in him, and he'd destroyed her, destroyed everything.

"I need to go," she muttered, her voice hollow, empty. "I need to get out of here."

Travis tried to reach for her, tried to hold her, but she pulled away, her body shakin', her mind screamin'. "Don't touch me!" she cried, her voice crackin', her eyes fillin' with tears. "Stay the fuck away from me!"

She stumbled out of the clinic, the world spinnin' around her, her heart poundin' in her chest. She didn't know where she was goin', didn't know what she was gonna do. All she knew was that she had to get away, had to get as far away from Travis, from the pain, from this fuckin bad news.

As she ran down the street, tears streamin' down her face, Carmen felt a sense of finality, a sense of loss, a sense of despair. She didn't know how to move forward or even if she could this was like a death sentence.

Chapter 18: Confrontation

Carmen paced back and forth in her small apartment, her mind racing, her heart pounding in her chest. She couldn't believe this was her life now. She couldn't believe how far she'd fallen, how much she'd lost. Travis's lies, his betrayals—they had cost her everything. Her health, her future, her peace of mind. She had trusted him, loved him, and he had destroyed her. And now, she had to face him, had to confront him, had to make him understand just how much he'd hurt her.

She heard the knock at the door, sharp and loud, echoing through the quiet room. She froze, her breath catching in her throat, her hands clenching into fists at her sides. She knew it was Travis, knew he was here to try and make things right, to try and fix what he'd broken. But it was too late. It was way too late for that.

With a deep breath, she walked over to the door, her heart heavy, her mind filled with anger and pain. She yanked it open, and there he was, standing in the hallway, looking as broken as she felt. His eyes were red, his face pale, his shoulders slumped. He looked like he hadn't slept in days, like he hadn't eaten, like the weight of his guilt was crushing him.

"Carmen, please," he began, his voice rough, filled with desperation. "I'm so sorry. I know I messed up. I know I hurt you. But please, let me explain. Let me try to make it right."

Carmen stared at him, her eyes hard, her jaw clenched. "Make it right?" she spat, her voice dripping with venom. "How the fuck are you gonna make this right, Travis? You ruined my life. You lied to me, cheated on me, and now I'm stuck with this... this disease because of you. How the hell do you fix that?"

Travis flinched, his face crumpling, his eyes filling with tears. "I know, Carmen. I know I fucked up. I know I hurt you more than anyone ever has. But I swear, I never meant for this to happen. I never wanted to hurt you."

Carmen felt a bitter laugh escape her lips, her hands shaking with rage. "Bullshit, Travis! You knew exactly what you were doing. You knew you were putting me at risk, and you didn't care. All you cared about was getting what you wanted, doing what you wanted. You never gave a damn about me!"

Travis took a step forward, his hands raised, his voice pleading. "That's not true, Carmen. I loved you. I still love you. I just... I was stupid. I was selfish. I didn't think. I didn't realize the consequences of my actions."

Carmen's eyes blazed with fury, her voice rising. "You didn't realize? You didn't realize? You're a grown-ass man, Travis! You knew exactly what you were doing. You just didn't care. You never cared."

Travis hung his head, his shoulders shaking, his tears falling freely. "I do care, Carmen. I care more than you'll ever know. I hate myself for what I've done, for what I've put you through. I'd give anything to take it back, to make it right."

Carmen shook her head, her heart breaking all over again. "You can't take it back, Travis. You can't fix this. You can't undo the damage you've done. I'm stuck with this for the rest of my life, and it's all because of you."

Travis fell to his knees, his hands clutching his head, his voice cracking with sobs. "I'm sorry, Carmen. I'm so fucking sorry. I wish I could go back, I wish I could change everything. But I can't. I can't, and I don't know what to do. I don't know how to make it right."

Carmen watched him, her eyes filled with tears, her chest heaving with emotion. She wanted to forgive him, wanted to believe that he was truly sorry, that he could change. But she couldn't. The damage was done. The trust was shattered. There was no going back.

"You can't make it right, Travis," she said softly, her voice trembling. "There's no fixing this. You've ruined everything. You've ruined us."

Travis looked up at her, his face streaked with tears, his eyes filled with despair. "Please, Carmen. Don't say that. Don't give up on me. I need you. I need you more than anything."

Carmen's heart ached, her mind racing. She wanted to reach out to him, to hold him, to tell him everything would be okay. But she couldn't. She couldn't keep lying to herself, couldn't keep pretending that things could ever go back to the way they were.

"It's too late, Travis," she said, her voice breaking. "It's too late for us. You've done too much damage. I can't keep doing this. I can't keep letting you hurt me."

Travis's face crumpled, his body shaking with sobs. "I know, Carmen. I know I've fucked up. But I love you. I love you more than anything. Please, just give me one more chance. Just one more."

Carmen shook her head, her tears falling freely. "I can't, Travis. I just... I can't. I have to move on. I have to find a way to live without you, to find myself again. I can't keep holding on to something that's killing me."

Travis reached out, his hands trembling, his eyes desperate. "Please, Carmen. Please don't leave me. I can't do this without you. I need you. I need you so much."

Carmen took a step back, her heart breaking, her mind screaming. She wanted to stay, wanted to believe that things could change, that they could find a way to make it work. But she knew better. She knew it was a fantasy, a dream that would never come true.

"I'm sorry, Travis," she whispered, her voice filled with pain. "But I can't. I have to go. I have to let you go."

Travis's face fell, his body collapsing to the floor, his sobs echoing through the empty room. "No, Carmen, please. Don't go. Don't leave me. I can't... I can't do this without you."

Carmen turned away, her heart shattering, her tears blinding her. She wanted to stay, wanted to hold him, to comfort him, to tell him everything would be okay. But she couldn't. She couldn't keep lying to herself, couldn't keep pretending that things could ever go back to the way they were.

She grabbed whatever he had and threw it in the hallway before telling him to get the fuck out, the door slamming shut behind him, the sound echoing through the hallway. She stood there for a moment, her body shaking, her mind numb. She couldn't believe this was happening.

She had to save herself, had to find a way to get healthy, to move on. She couldn't keep holding on to the past, couldn't keep letting Travis drag her down and ruin her life.

Chapter 19: Acceptance and Farewell

Carmen had walked away from Travis for good after everything that had happened. She'd had every reason to leave him behind, to let him face his consequences alone. But when she heard how bad he was doing, how quickly his health was declining, she couldn't stay away. As much as she wanted to hate him, a part of her still cared, still couldn't abandon him, not when he needed someone the most.

Travis's health went downhill fast. He was already thin and frail from the HIV, but now he was wasting away, his skin pale and his eyes sunken deep into his face. He barely ate, barely moved from the bed. The strong, confident man he'd once been was gone, replaced by a shadow of his former self, broken and fragile.

Carmen visited him every other day in the hospice. The place smelled like sickness and despair, and the sight of him lying there, hooked up to tubes and machines, made her chest tighten. She'd never seen him so weak, so vulnerable. It was like lookin' at a stranger.

"Hey, Carmen," Travis croaked one day as she sat by his bedside, his voice barely a whisper. "Thanks for bein' here. I know I don't deserve it."

Carmen forced a small smile, though it hurt to look at him. "It's okay, Travis. I just... I couldn't leave you like this."

Travis closed his eyes, his chest rising and falling with each labored breath. "I'm so sorry, Carmen. For everything. For all the lies, all the bullshit. I never meant to hurt you."

Carmen's throat tightened, tears welling up in her eyes. "I know, Travis. I know you didn't mean to, but you did. You hurt me more than anyone ever has. You broke me."

Travis turned his head to look at her, his eyes full of pain and regret. "I wish I could take it all back. I wish I could make it right. But it's too late for that now. I just... I just wanted to tell you that I love you, Carmen. I always have, even if I never showed it right."

Carmen nodded, biting her lip to keep from crying. She wanted to tell him she loved him too, that despite everything, she still cared. But she couldn't. The words wouldn't come. All she could do was sit there, holding his hand, feeling the warmth slowly fading from his skin.

As the days passed, Travis got worse. The doctors said it wouldn't be long now, that his body was shutting down, giving up the fight. Carmen stayed by his side, refusing to leave him alone, even when he was unconscious, even when he couldn't speak. She couldn't abandon him, not after everything they'd been through.

One night, as she sat there, her head resting on the edge of the bed, she felt his hand squeeze hers, weak but there. She looked up, seeing his eyes open, staring at her with a clarity she hadn't seen in weeks.

"Carmen," he whispered, his voice barely audible. "Thank you... for everything. I'm... I'm so sorry."

Carmen's heart shattered, tears streaming down her face. "I forgive you, Travis. I forgive you."

Travis gave her a weak smile, his eyes closing, his grip on her hand loosening. And then he was gone. Just like that, the life drained out of him, leaving his body still and cold. Carmen sat there, staring at him, her mind numb, her heart heavy with a mix of sadness, anger, and a strange sense of relief.

She knew she should feel something more, something deeper, but all she felt was empty, like all the pain, all the anger had been sucked out of her, leaving nothing behind. She had loved him, hated him, forgiven him, and now he was gone. And all she could think was that it was finally over.

The days after Travis's death were a blur. There were arrangements to be made, people to call, things to take care of. Carmen went through the motions, doing what needed to be done, but her mind was somewhere else, lost in a fog of memories and regrets.

She thought about all the good times, the moments when Travis had made her laugh, made her feel special, made her believe in love. She thought about all the bad times, the lies, the betrayals, the pain. She thought about the life they could have had, the future they could have built, if things had been different.

But things weren't different. This was her reality now. Travis was gone, and she was left to pick up the pieces of her shattered life, to find a way to move forward, to heal.

On the day of the funeral, Carmen stood by his grave, watching as they lowered his coffin into the ground. The sky was gray and overcast, a light drizzle falling, soaking through her clothes, but she barely felt it. She stood there, staring at the hole in the ground, feeling like she was burying a part of herself along with him.

As the crowd started to disperse, people offering their condolences, their words of comfort, Carmen stayed behind, needing a moment alone, a moment to say goodbye.

"I don't know if you can hear me, Travis," she said softly, her voice breaking, tears streaming down her face. "But I hope you're at peace now. I hope you've found whatever it was you were looking for. I loved you, even if you never really knew how to love me back."

She knelt down, placing a single rose on top of the coffin, her hand lingering there for a moment, feeling the cold, hard wood beneath her fingers. "Goodbye, Travis," she whispered, her voice barely audible. "I hope you find peace."

As she stood up, turning to leave, she felt a strange sense of calm wash over her, a sense of acceptance. She knew she couldn't change the past, couldn't undo the mistakes, the pain, but she could choose to move forward, to live her life, to find her own happiness.

She walked away from the grave, her head held high, her heart heavy but determined. She knew she had a long road ahead, knew she still had a lot of healing to do, but she was ready. Ready to focus on herself, to put herself first, to never let anyone take advantage of her kindness and naivety again.

As she left the cemetery, the rain pouring down around her, Carmen felt a flicker of hope, a spark of something new, something stronger. She didn't know what the future held, didn't know where life was headed, but she knew she was going to be okay. She knew she was going to make it, one step at a time.

Chapter 20: Moving Forward

Carmen woke up to a new day, the sun streaming through the curtains of her small apartment, casting a warm glow across the room. For the first time in what felt like forever, she felt a sense of calm, a sense of peace. Travis was gone, and with him went the chaos, the lies, the heartbreak. It was a strange feeling, being alone again, but it was also liberating. She was free, finally free to live her life on her own terms, to be who she wanted to be.

She got up, stretching her arms above her head, feeling the tension leave her muscles. She had a long day ahead of her, a day filled with classes and work, but she was ready. She was ready to take on whatever came her way, ready to face the challenges, the obstacles, the struggles. She had been through hell and back, and she wasn't about to let anything stop her now.

As she got dressed, pulling on a pair of jeans and a simple blouse, she thought about how far she'd come, how much she'd changed. She wasn't the same girl she used to be, the shy, demure girl who let everyone walk all over her. She was stronger now, tougher, more confident. She knew what she wanted, and she wasn't afraid to go after it.

She grabbed her backpack, slinging it over her shoulder, and headed out the door. As she walked down the street, the sounds of the city buzzing around her, she felt a sense of determination, a sense of purpose. She was going to make something of herself, going to prove to everyone, especially herself, that she was more than just a girl who fell for the wrong guy.

Her first stop was the community college where she'd been taking classes part-time. She had taken a break after everything with Travis, but now she was ready to get back into it, ready to finish what she'd started. She walked into the registration office, her head held high, her heart racing with anticipation.

"Hi, I'd like to re-enroll in my courses," she said to the woman behind the counter, her voice steady, her eyes focused.

The woman looked up, smiling. "Of course, let me pull up your file. It's good to see you back, Carmen. We missed you."

Carmen smiled, feeling a warmth spread through her chest. It felt good to be back, to be doing something positive, something for herself. She filled out the necessary forms, signed on the dotted line, and before she knew it, she was a student again, ready to take on her studies, to learn, to grow.

After leaving the college, she decided to stop by her family's house. It had been a while since she'd seen them, really seen them, and she knew she needed to reconnect, to let them know she was okay, that she was moving forward.

As she walked up the front steps, the familiar creak of the wood under her feet, she took a deep breath, steadying herself. She knocked on the door, her heart pounding in her chest, her mind racing with thoughts of what she would say, how she would explain everything.

The door swung open, and there was her mama, standing in the doorway, her eyes wide with surprise. "Carmen! Baby, what are you doin' here?"

Carmen smiled, feeling tears prick at the corners of her eyes. "I just... I just wanted to see y'all. I wanted to let you know I'm okay."

Her mama pulled her into a tight hug, her arms wrapping around her, holding her close. "Oh, Carmen, we've been so worried about you. We didn't know what to do, didn't know how to help you."

Carmen hugged her back, her tears falling freely now, her heart aching with the love she felt for her family. "I know, Mama. I'm sorry. I'm so sorry for everything. I just... I had to go through it. I had to figure it out on my own."

Her mama pulled back, cupping Carmen's face in her hands, her eyes filled with tears. "We just want you to be happy, Carmen. We just want you to find your way, to be the strong, beautiful woman we know you are."

Carmen nodded, her heart swelling with emotion. "I'm gettin' there, Mama. I'm gettin' there."

They spent time talking, catching up, laughing, and crying. Carmen felt a weight lift off her shoulders, felt a sense of relief wash over her. She realized how much she'd missed them, how much she needed them. They were her rock, her foundation, and she was grateful to have them in her life.

After leaving her family's house, Carmen decided to reach out to some of her old friends, the ones she'd lost touch with during her time with Travis. She knew it wouldn't be easy, knew there were some bridges she needed to rebuild, but she was ready to try, ready to make amends.

She called Mariah, her best friend from way back, the one who'd been there for her through thick and thin, until she'd pushed her away, caught up in the whirlwind of Travis's world. She was nervous, unsure of what to say, but when Mariah picked up, her voice warm and familiar, Carmen felt a flicker of hope.

"Hey, Mariah. It's Carmen," she said softly, her voice trembling. "I just... I just wanted to say what's up? I miss you. I really do."

There was a pause on the other end of the line, and for a moment, Carmen thought she might hang up, might tell her to fuck off. But then she heard Mariah's voice, soft and forgiving. "I miss you too, Carmen. And I'm glad you called. I've been thinkin' about you, wonderin' how you were doin'."

Carmen's heart swelled with relief, a smile spreading across her face. "I'm makin it, Mariah. I'm tryin'. I just... I want to make things right. I want to be a better friend, a better person."

Mariah laughed softly, her voice filled with warmth. "I know you do, Carmen. And I'm here for you. I always have been. Let's get together soon, okay? We've got a lot to catch up on."

Carmen agreed, feeling a weight lift off her shoulders, feeling a sense of peace settle over her. She knew she still had a long way to go, still had a lot of healing to do, but she was ready. She was ready to move forward, to start fresh, to live her life on her own terms.

Over the next few weeks, Carmen threw herself into her studies, focusing on her classes, her work, her health, her goals. She reconnected with old friends, made new ones, surrounded herself with people who lifted her up, who supported her, who believed in her. She started going to therapy, working through her pain, her trauma, her past. She took up yoga, started running, taking care of her body, her mind, her spirit.

She felt stronger, more confident, more alive than she had in years. She wasn't the same girl she used to be, the girl who let everyone walk all over her, who put others' needs before her own, who believed she wasn't enough. She was different now. She was a warrior, a survivor, a diva in her own right.

One day, as she was walking through the neighborhood, she ran into an old neighbor, Mrs. Jenkins, an older woman who'd known her since she was a kid. Mrs. Jenkins looked at her, her eyes widening in surprise. "Carmen? Is that you? You look... different."

Carmen smiled, feeling a sense of pride swell in her chest. "Yeah, Mrs. Jenkins, it's me. I guess you could say I've changed a bit."

Mrs. Jenkins nodded, her eyes filled with admiration. "Well, whatever you're doing, keep it up. You look good, girl. You look like you're ready to take on the world."

Carmen laughed, feeling a warmth spread through her. "I am, Mrs. Jenkins. I am."

Don't miss out!

Visit the website below and you can sign up to receive emails whenever Rachael Reed publishes a new book. There's no charge and no obligation.

https://books2read.com/r/B-A-WXARB-KCHYE

BOOKS2READ

Connecting independent readers to independent writers.

[2]

Sis: A Tale of Power and Betrayal

In the heart of Richmond's unforgiving streets, Jasmine has clawed her way to the top, ruling her empire with an iron fist and a sharp mind. Born into the harsh realities of the ghetto, she turned to the drug game to escape poverty, becoming a formidable force in a world dominated by betrayal, violence, and survival. But power comes at a price, and the streets are always hungry for blood.

Jasmine's journey is one of relentless ambition and ruthless determination. From small-time hustling to partnering with the notorious Dre, she learned the rules of the game the hard way. When Dre's betrayal threatened everything she had built, Jasmine took

---

1. https://books2read.com/u/mZlxoR

2. https://books2read.com/u/mZlxoR

matters into her own hands, proving that she's not one to be crossed. Now, as the queen of Richmond's underworld, she faces new enemies and internal power struggles that could bring her empire crashing down.

As Jasmine fights to maintain her reign, she grapples with the personal cost of her decisions. Guilt, regret, and the loss of innocence weigh heavily on her, even as she seeks redemption by giving back to her community. But the streets are relentless, and new threats emerge, testing her strategic brilliance and unyielding resolve.

In a world where trust is a luxury and betrayal lurks around every corner, Jasmine must navigate the treacherous waters of the drug game with cunning and ferocity. The final showdown with a new rival threatens to dismantle everything she has fought for, leading to an explosive climax that will decide the future of her reign.

Sis is a gripping tale of power, survival, and the brutal realities of urban life. With its gritty dialogue, dark undertones, and relentless pace, this novel plunges you into the heart of the streets, where every decision can mean the difference between life and death. Jasmine's story is one of fierce loyalty, calculated moves, and the constant struggle to stay on top in a world that never truly lets go.

Also by Rachael Reed

Sis
Sis 2 Blood on the Streets

Standalone
Codefendant
Codefendant
Once a Cheater
Once a Cheater
Passport Bro
What Happens in Prison
Preference
Sprinkle Sprinkle
Championship Bad
Street Exodus
Street Exodus
Street Royalty
Pawns of Power
SIS
Cartel Bloodline
Get Money Girls
Skip the Games
Til Death Do Us Part

Backpage Hustle
Link in Bio
The Virgin and The Kingpin
A Gangsta's Heart
Boosters
Can't Turn a Hoe Into a Housewife
Better you Than Me
Wig Dealer: How to Start Your wig Business
Trail Ride Blues
Demure Diva